Oedipus at Palm Springs

A Five Lesbian Brothers Play
written by
Maureen Angelos,
Dominique Dibbell,
Peg Healy,
and Lisa Kron

A SAMUEL FRENCH ACTING EDITION

FOUNDED 1830

SAMUELFRENCH.COM
SAMUELFRENCH-LONDON.CO.UK

FOR PRODUCTION ENQUIRIES

UNITED STATES AND CANADA
Info@SamuelFrench.com
1-866-598-8449

UNITED KINGDOM AND EUROPE
Plays@SamuelFrench-London.co.uk
020-7255-4302

Each title is subject to availability from Samuel French, depending
upon country of performance. Please be aware that *OEDIPUS AT PALM
SPRINGS* may not be licensed by Samuel French in your territory.
Professional and amateur producers should contact the nearest Samuel
French office or licensing partner to verify availability.

MUSIC USE NOTE

Licensees are solely responsible for obtaining formal written permission from copyright owners to use copyrighted music in the performance of this play and are strongly cautioned to do so. If no such permission is obtained by the licensee, then the licensee must use only original music that the licensee owns and controls. Licensees are solely responsible and liable for all music clearances and shall indemnify the copyright owners of the play(s) and their licensing agent, Samuel French, against any costs, expenses, losses and liabilities arising from the use of music by licensees. Please contact the appropriate music licensing authority in your territory for the rights to any incidental music.

IMPORTANT BILLING AND CREDIT REQUIREMENTS

If you have obtained performance rights to this title, please refer to your licensing agreement for important billing and credit requirements.

OEDIPUS AT PALM SPRINGS was first produced by the New York Theatre Workshop in July 2005. The performance was directed by Leigh Silverman, with sets by David Korins, costumes by Miranda Hoffman, lighting by M.L. Geiger, and sound design by John Gromada. The production stage manager was Martha Donaldson. The cast was as follows:

JONI	Babs Davy
CON	Lisa Kron
FRAN	Maureen Angelos
PRIN	Dominique Dibbell
TERRI	Peg Healey

CHARACTERS

PRIN – (short for PRINCESS, early 50s*) Terri's lover, a handsome stone butch and a highly successful/wealthy entrepreneur with a penchant for the ladies and booze. Loves and is devoted to Terri.

TERRI – (mid-30s*) Prin's lover. A younger, post-gay lesbian and a student. A devoted lover, dependent on Prin.

CON – (40s) A feminist lesbian. Fran's life partner, co-parent of Basil, an industrious hospital administrator, sexually frustrated.

FRAN – (40s) Soft butch. Con's life partner, bio-mom of Basil. Ex-business partner and long-time devoted friend of Prin. Sexually disinterested.

JONI – (60s) Blind manager of Casitas Bonitas, painter and soothsayer. One thirty-eighth Native American.

NOTE: The age difference between Prin and Terri must be 15 years or more.

SETTING

CASITAS BONITAS

A private, walled-in women's desert resort. Set should include: two private bungalows, a swimming pool, a barbecue/dining area, an entry gate.

OTHER LOCATIONS:
SHAME ON THE MOON, a restaurant
COCKATIELS, a night club
PALM CANYON DRIVE, outside the night club

TIME

2005

Casitas Bonitas Courtyard, Friday Evening

(A private, walled-in, women's desert resort. Several casitas – numbered bungalows – are decorated in faux Native-American style.)

(k.d. lang's "Constant Craving" plays at a level just high enough so that it can't be ignored and just low enough that you can't quite listen to it.*)

(JONI, *the hotel manager, pushes a cleaning cart upstage. Her hair is white and shorn close, except for a long braid that drops all the way to her butt and is tied off with a bell and some feathers. She is naked except for sunglasses, a full-body tan that can best be described as "desert crinkle" and a cell phone that is strapped around her waist.)*

(Her keys jingle as she works quickly, unlocking doors and dropping off clean towels and welcome baskets.)

(After a few moments, a buzzer rings.)

JONI. Mother! Fuck!

(She crosses to the intercom. For the first time, we see that she is blind.)

JONI. *(into intercom)* Yeah?

(A woman's voice responds through the speaker.)

CON. *(offstage) (over the intercom)* Hey, Joni, it's Con.

JONI. Who?

CON. *(offstage)* Con! Con and Fran!

(JONI *buzzes them in then grabs a gauzy dress from a pile of dirty towels and pulls it over her head.)*

---

* Please see Music Use Note on Page Three.

(**CON** *and* **FRAN** *enter with tons of baggage.*)

CON & FRAN. Oh, it's so beautiful. Isn't it?

> *(then)*

> Joni. Hi.

JONI. Greetings.

CON. Look at this place! We got here at the perfect time. The light is magical. Isn't it beautiful, Fran.

FRAN. Looks great. Did you do some renovating?

JONI. Time passes. Some things fall away. Others take their place.

CON. I don't know what it is about walking through that gate.

FRAN. I know! Palm Canyon Drive is right out there. But this side of the wall feels like another world.

CON. It's so great to be somewhere we can just be ourselves.

FRAN. Yeah.

> (**CON** *gives* **FRAN** *a peck and a little squeeze.*)

CON. Are Prin and Terri here yet?

JONI. No.

CON. Really? Good.

FRAN. I've got to pump. My breasts are killing me.

CON. We have a kid now, Joni. He's three and, believe it or not, this is the first time we've been away from him.

FRAN. You'd love him. He's a pisser. He's so smart.

CON. He can count to eleven…

CON & FRAN. *(together)* …in Spanish.

JONI. Don't like children anymore.

> *(then)*

> You're in the Jacuzzi room.

CON. *(psyched)* That is very good news.

> *(They follow* **JONI** *to their door.)*

FRAN. Prin got us the Jacuzzi room?

CON. She said she wanted this weekend to be really special.

(They follow JONI to their casita. JONI opens the door. They enter.)

(FRAN does the heavy work of moving the luggage while CON unpacks a few frills to add ambience to their room – a sexy fabric for the bed, candles, incense, etc.)

CON. Fran. Fran. It's like a honeymoon hideaway.

JONI. Check out the services binder. There's some new spa treatments we're offering.

CON. Do you still have that German lady who does the facials?

JONI. Belgian. No, she goes back to Europe during the off-season. But I'm doing key readings.

FRAN. Key readings?

JONI. I toss your keys then read the energy. It's very effective.

(CON emerges from the casita.)

FRAN. Maybe we should try it, hon. Figure out what the fuck is wrong with us.

CON. *(nervous laugh)* Fran!

FRAN. *(to JONI)* Nothing's wrong with us.

CON. Nothing's wrong with us.

(JONI stares at them, inscrutable.)

(CON gets increasingly uncomfortable as JONI remains mute.)

CON. We're having a little sexual dysfunction, but that's very normal for a couple after their first child. Maybe our lack of sex – that's our problem, lack of sex – maybe it's gone on a little long. Longer than usual.

FRAN. This weekend's really going to help.

CON. Yeah.

JONI. I'll get your muffin basket.

(JONI leaves.)

CON. Why did I say all that? God, she's so inscrutable.

FRAN. Shh. She's blind, not deaf.

CON. I said inscrutable, not rude and bizarre. And please can we not broadcast all our personal business.

FRAN. Me? You were the one blabbering on.

CON. Yeah, I know. But you just stood there. You could've stopped me. Hey, I really don't want you talking with Prin and Terri about our sex life this weekend, okay?

FRAN. Okay.

(FRAN *gets a beer from the mini cooler they brought.*)

CON. Where are you going?

FRAN. The girls are going to be here pretty soon. I want to meet them.

CON. Is that a beer?

FRAN. Yeah.

(FRAN *goes out to the courtyard.*)

CON. Fran?

FRAN. What?

(*then*)

Is it the beer? I just thought since we were away I might have a few.

CON. Honey, I need you not to disappear on me this weekend.

FRAN. Alright, then. I won't drink the beer.

CON. That would be good. And I won't drink either. That way we'll be able to show up for each other this weekend and work on what we discussed with Devra.

FRAN. Totally.

CON. Refocusing.

FRAN. Refocusing.

CON. On what?

FRAN. On our sexual connection?

CON. Yes, that. But mostly on each other. On being in our relationship, prioritizing that.

FRAN. I was close, though, right?

CON. So that's what we're going to do?

FRAN. That is totally what we're going to do. So. Should we do our exercises now?

CON. Out here?

FRAN. Sure. No one else is here. We can do the one.

CON. Okay.

(They hug stiffly.)

CON. Are you doing the breathing?

FRAN. Yeah.

(They continue hugging in silence.)

CON. I don't know if you're supposed to be resting your head on my shoulder like that.

*(**FRAN** lifts her head and tries to figure out what to do with it. She leans it against **CON**'s head.)*

CON. Didn't Devra say that we're supposed to each be leaning "into" each other but not "on" each other?

FRAN. Am I leaning?

CON. A little bit.

FRAN. I'm just hugging you.

CON. Okay.

(then)

Ow.

FRAN. What?

CON. Nothing. Just keep hugging until we're relaxed.

*(The Main Gate opens and **PRINCESS** enters. She is a handsome stone butch in her early 50s.)*

PRIN. Caught cha!

*(**CON** and **FRAN** break their hug.)*

PRIN. Easy on the nookie, you two. The weekend's just getting started.

FRAN. Hey!

*(**PRIN** gives **FRAN** a big bear hug.)*

PRIN. You beat me, you dog. You hit that traffic around Corona?

FRAN. Yeah. I was going to take the 15 up to the 60, but Con was like, no, let's stay on the 91.

PRIN. Fucking 91. Backed up to Riverside.

(While still talking to **FRAN**, *she goes to* **CON** *and takes her in her arms.)*

And how is the most gorgeous mommy in Rancho Mission Viejo?

(She dips **CON**.*)*

CON. *(fanning herself)* Hot.

PRIN. I'll say.

CON. Better not let Terri hear that.

(then, concerned)

Is she doing okay?

PRIN. Yeah, she's okay. She's a trooper. I've got a fantastic weekend planned.

CON. It's good we're here. It's always hard – the first birthday without your mom.

PRIN. Don't make a big deal though, okay? She just wants to have a good time.

FRAN. Oh sure.

CON. Oh, we wouldn't.

*(***TERRI** *enters.)*

TERRI. Hi, you guys!

CON. *(all super sympathetic)* Hey, kiddo.

*(***CON** *and* **TERRI** *hug.)*

FRAN. How you holdin' up, Ter?

TERRI. *(big sigh)* I'm okay.

(beat)

I'm really okay, you guys. How are you? I'm so glad to see you.

CON & FRAN. *(still focused on Terri)* We're fine. We're good.

TERRI. We're going to have a fantastic time. Okay? That's what I want for my birthday, okay?

(changing the subject)

Con, when did you do that to your hair? You look amazing.

CON. You've seen this.

TERRI. No, I haven't.

CON. I had it done three months ago.

PRIN. We haven't laid eyes on you since what – the Rusty Pelican?

FRAN. No way, that was around Easter.

CON. I think she's right. We were going to do that Sparks thing but we had to back out.

FRAN. Basil had that reaction to kiwi.

CON. She gave him kiwi. She gave a three year old kiwi!

FRAN. I didn't know it was on some list of reactive foods.

PRIN. Yeah, whatever. The point is it's not easy getting you two out of that hermetically sealed nursery.

TERRI. Prin, stop. You both look beautiful. Fran, you look so voluptuous and gorgeous.

(FRAN shifts from foot to foot uncomfortably.)

How's B?

FRAN. I miss him so much already.

CON. He's good. He's at his grandma's.

FRAN. I can't believe you got us the fucking Jacuzzi room.

PRIN. Jacuzzi room? No, that's some kind of mistake. I didn't get you the Jacuzzi room.

(CON and FRAN look at each other awkwardly.)

FRAN. Oh, we…Joni said…

PRIN. I hope you didn't stain the sheets yet.

FRAN. No, we…

PRIN. I'm just kidding you. I got you the Jacuzzi room.

CON. Jesus! Prin!

FRAN. Next time's on us.

PRIN. Hey, I like the new Saab. Very nice.

FRAN. Yeah, Con let me have it.

CON. I drive the minivan.

PRIN. Job treating you okay? Ketterwelter busting your ass?

FRAN. Oh yeah. Doug's great. It's good. Good.

CON. Are you kidding? The whole department worships her.

PRIN. I got a great deal going down in these condos in Phoenix. Sure you don't want to jump in with me?

FRAN. Can't do that anymore. I've got enough ups and down with the kid and all.

PRIN. Fen Yan is giving me a 30-year fixed rate at 3.5.

FRAN. 3.5? Really?

(CON and TERRI share a look.)

TERRI. Hey! Woo-hoo! Masters of the universe! We're on vacation, remember?

CON. First rule of the weekend – no business talk after sunset.

PRIN. Con has spoken.

FRAN. Sorry, babe. You're right. I'm here to leave all that behind.

(JONI enters.)

JONI. Princess. Good to have you back. My oldest customer.

(She holds out her hand. PRINCESS shakes it.)

PRIN. Aw, come on. 52's not that old. What are you doing here this time of year? Aren't you usually on a treasure hunt or…what are those things you do?

JONI. Vision Quest. No, I couldn't go this year because Jorel and Tiny are in Guatemala on a buying trip so they asked me to stay through August. So, here I am. Casita 26, right?

(JONI pulls out her keys. Then when she senses TERRI, freezes. There is a pause.)

TERRI. Hi. My name's Terri.

CON. She knows you, Terri.

TERRI. No, we've never met.

CON. You've never met Joni?

PRIN. She wasn't here when we came before.

(**TERRI** *extends her hand.* **JONI** *doesn't take it.*)

JONI. Is she your…?

PRIN. She's my girlfriend.

(**TERRI** *drops her hand.*)

JONI. No. This is someone else.

PRIN. Nope. I'm pretty sure this is my girlfriend.

JONI. Hm.

FRAN. She's brought so many girls here over the years you're probably just confused.

PRIN. Terri and I have been together for seven years. It's her birthday. Remember, I told you that over the phone?

JONI. Today is her birthday?

TERRI. Sunday, actually. Sunday's my birthday.

(**JONI** *laughs.*)

TERRI. What's so funny?

JONI. Birthdays are funny things. How sometimes you can forget your own birthday.

PRIN. I do that. I forget if Terri doesn't remind me.

JONI. It looks like you four have the place to yourselves this weekend.

CON. Yeah. We're the only ones crazy enough to come to the desert in the middle of August.

JONI. I think it's the best time to come. Only the strong remain.

TERRI. Joni, I was wondering if you had some information about the Painted Canyons?

JONI. The painted canyons can never be fully known.

TERRI. I just meant, the hours and stuff.

JONI. There is a brochure in your binder.

TERRI. Oh. Thanks.

JONI. What are you looking for?

TERRI. Um, looking for?

JONI. You're looking for something…

TERRI. I…

JONI. A roadrunner?

TERRI. Well, yes, I'd like to see a roadrunner.

JONI. *(laughs)* You won't find it there. Here. Take your muffins.

> *(JONI exits.)*

> *(FRAN makes a space ship sound.)*

TERRI. What was that?

CON. You'll get used to her. She does readings and stuff. It can be kind of fun.

FRAN. Isn't she like 1/38th Blackfoot or something?

PRIN. How can you be 1/38th anything?

TERRI. I just asked her a simple question.

PRIN. Readings, predictions. You make your own bed and you lie in it, that's what I say. What say we hit the pool and drown ourselves in some margaritas? I got the good stuff.

FRAN. Sounds great!

CON. Fran?

FRAN. Oh. Okay, well.

CON. I think we're going to turn in early. It's been a long week.

PRIN. You're kidding me. It's only 8:30!

CON. We're on "mommy time."

PRIN. Oh, I get it. These two get five minutes away from the kid and BANG! *(to FRAN, wink, wink)* No worries, pal. Have a good "rest."

> *(TERRI grabs PRIN by the hand.)*

TERRI. Come on, baby. I'm feeling a little "tired" myself.

CON. See you in the morning.

PRIN. Right! Morning. Fran, we have tee-off at 7:30. You girls have the whole morning at the outlets. Don't spend too much. Back here for BBQ. Then Sunday is birthday, birthday, birthday. Dinner at Shame on the Moon.

CON. Wow! You really do have the whole weekend planned.

PRIN. That's just the beginning. 'Night folks!

Prin and Terri's Casita

(PRIN and TERRI enter. They kiss, deeply. TERRI breaks it off.)

TERRI. I can't believe it's been so long since we've actually seen Fran and Con.

PRIN. Who?

(TERRI pushes PRIN off.)

TERRI. You devil.

PRIN. I can't get used to that rack on Fran.

TERRI. Go easy on her, Prin. She's a little fragile, I think.

PRIN. The mommy thing's makin' her all soft.

TERRI. You love your friend, Fran.

PRIN. Do not.

TERRI. You've missed her.

PRIN. Have not.

TERRI. Be sweet with her. She thinks you don't approve of her life with a kid and a desk job.

PRIN. I don't.

TERRI. I'm just saying. You be sweet.

PRIN. Okay, I'll be nice. I'll be like – No, tell me again? How many times did Basil poop today? I'm really interested.

TERRI. You know what's insane?

PRIN. What?

TERRI. That kid is crazy for you.

PRIN. What can I say?

(grabbing TERRI's ass)

The youngsters love me.

TERRI. Yes we do.

(PRIN pushes TERRI on to the bed. They kiss. Then…)

Before I forget I need to call this guy back.

PRIN. Which guy?

TERRI. That detective who found Antonia's mother.

PRIN. I don't know who that is.

TERRI. Yes you do. Antonia, from that group. She's been looking for her mom for like 12 years. This guy is amazing and he found her in, like, a couple of weeks and Antonia flew to Houston and met her mother. She has a brother and two sisters now. When she came back she was so changed. She said she felt whole for the first time in her life.

(PRIN gets up and goes to the fridge.)

I'm sorry.

PRIN. For what?

TERRI. You're so irritated with me.

PRIN. I'm not irritated with you. I'm just getting some ice.

TERRI. I know you think it's a bad idea for me to look for my birth mother.

PRIN. I don't have an opinion about it, sweetheart.

TERRI. But you think I'm too focused on it.

PRIN. I think you had a great mother.

TERRI. I know. I did. I had a wonderful mother. But when Betty died – I can't explain it. It feels like it opened up this hole in me that nothing can fill.

(heading PRIN off)

And don't go making one of your jokes.

PRIN. Do you think maybe you just need to give yourself some more time to deal with Betty's death?

TERRI. It's been six months. It's not getting better. I feel like I'm not attached to anything. Like I don't belong anywhere. What have I done with myself? I pissed away my twenties.

PRIN. Who didn't?

TERRI. You didn't. You started how many businesses? And Con and Fran didn't.

PRIN. You're gonna get your degree in a few months.

TERRI. But does the world really need another communications major?

PRIN. Baby – look at me. How 'bout giving yourself a little break? Huh?

TERRI. You're right. You brought me out here for a beautiful birthday weekend and I'm going to have one. I'm putting away my cell phone and I'm focusing on you and our friends. But mostly I'm going to focus on you.

PRIN. That's my girl.

TERRI. Oh, Prin, was I always this touchy?

PRIN. I don't know. Let me touch you.

TERRI. Come on, I didn't used to be like this. Did you see how I was with that crazy Joni? She totally spooked me.

PRIN. Yeah, well. She's spooky.

TERRI. Prin. What would I do without you?

PRIN. Perish.

TERRI. I would.

(*then*)

God. How do you do that to me? Is this my birthday present. Because it's really good what you're doing right now.

PRIN. No, it's even better.

TERRI. Better than this?

PRIN. Yeah, I'm going to go to the mall and get you some socks or something.

TERRI. You beast! Just for that I'm going to go sleep in Fran and Con's room.

PRIN. Oh, don't interrupt them. Now that they're away from that kid, those two are going at it like porn stars just finishing a prison sentence.

(**PRIN** *throws* **TERRI** *on the bed and climbs on top of her like a porn stud.* **TERRI** *squeals with delight.*)

Fran and Con's Casita

(CON is lying on the bed. FRAN is sitting next to her and stroking her lightly with one hand.)

FRAN. How does that feel?

CON. Nice.

(A timer goes off.)

FRAN. So that was nice?

CON. Yeah. It's interesting that you just use the one hand.

FRAN. Good interesting or bad interesting?

CON. Neither. Just interesting. Feathery.

FRAN. Feathery, yeah. That's what I was going for.

CON. Oh. Well, it was good then. It was really feathery.

FRAN. Did you not like it? I'm not clear on what you're saying to me.

CON. It was good. It was fine. It was really nice. It's just interesting to me because I use both hands and massage more but you're doing something different. It felt a little like you weren't paying that much attention but now that I understand you're doing the feather thing it's fine.

(She gets up.)

Want some water?

FRAN. Sure.

CON. Prin and Terri seem good.

FRAN. Yeah. Always at it.

CON. It's almost too much, you know? Like, if you have to flaunt it, you haven't got it.

FRAN. Oh, I think they have a pretty good sex life.

CON. Yeah.

FRAN. They have some connection.

CON. Well, they're still getting to know each other.

FRAN. After seven years?

CON. Yeah. Give them another decade and we'll see how hot they are.

FRAN. Oh, totally.

CON. *(then)* Okay. So, your turn. I do you.

(**FRAN** *lies down on her stomach.*)

Honey?

FRAN. Umhm.

CON. I think you need to turn over. This is the part where we add in the breast touching.

FRAN. Oh, no. I don't think I can do that.

CON. I won't do it in a sexual way. I know it's hard to feel sexual when you're nursing.

FRAN. Yeah. I'm more comfortable this way.

CON. Honey. That's hard for me. Honey? It feels really rejecting to me.

FRAN. I'm not rejecting you, honey. I just don't want to have my tits touched in that way.

CON. I'm not going to inappropriately sexualize you but I want to be close to you. I want to share this experience with you.

FRAN. Okay.

(**FRAN** *turns face up.* **CON** *touches her breasts through her clothes.*)

CON. How is this for you?

FRAN. It's so uncomfortable.

(**CON** *gives a deep, irritated sigh.*)

What? I'm sorry. It is.

CON. No, I know.

(**CON** *gets up and starts straightening up the room.*)

FRAN. Con.

CON. What?

FRAN. Con. Come on. Come over here and let's talk about this.

CON. What? I love your tits and I'm not allowed to touch them and it makes me really sad!

FRAN. Oh, honey. I'm so sorry. I do understand. I just don't know what to do. I mean, it is really intense while I'm breast feeding. It's like my breasts aren't for sex. They're for food.

CON. Do you think we should try again to wean Basil?

FRAN. Really? You think so?

CON. No, never mind. I'm the bad mommy.

FRAN. Con, don't do that. You're not the bad mommy.

CON. I'm the bad, selfish mommy. He is three, Fran.

FRAN. Yeah, but I think he's still really... It's a big thing for him still.

CON. You're right.

FRAN. Don't be mad.

CON. I'm feeling a little desperate. Do you understand that?

FRAN. Of course I do, honey. I love you so much.

CON. Then kiss me, Fran.

(FRAN *gives her a kiss.*)

Kiss me like you mean it, Fran.

(FRAN *kisses her a little deeper.*)

CON. Make love to me, Fran.

FRAN. Oh, Con. I can't. Not right now.

(CON *pulls away.*)

Honey, I'm just not in that place.

CON. It's been four years, Fran.

FRAN. I know, honey. We'll work on it. We are working on it.

CON. No, you're not listening to me. Four years. Four. Four. Four. Four. Years since we last had sex —

FRAN. We'll work on it, honey.

CON. We've been in couple's counseling for six years. We've been in sex counseling since last November. No, Fran, no. No more processing. It's not working. You need to figure out how to give me some sex.

FRAN. Okay, okay. I'll go into individual counseling. I can wean Basil. You're right. It's time. I'll figure it out, honey. Just give me a little more time.

CON. You have till Sunday.

FRAN. Sunday?

CON. I'm not kidding.

FRAN. Not kidding about what?

CON. This weekend, Fran. You have this weekend to figure it out and give me some sex.

FRAN. But Con…

CON. Figure it out.

FRAN. Honey?

CON. I'm going in the bathroom and I'm going to jerk off. That's the other thing that's going to change. I'm not going to keep sneaking around. We both know I masturbate all the time. I'm desperate for sex. I know I seem insane. I can't help it. I can't keep pretending that I don't have any needs. I cannot continue in this relationship the way it is. I love you, Franny, and I love Basil but I just can't do it.

(She exits into the bathroom and slams the door.)

Courtyard, Later that Night

(Late night. **FRAN** *is awake in her casita. She steps out into the night. She dips her toe in the pool.)*

PRIN. So. Did you get any?

FRAN. Prin?

*(***FRAN*** *turns to see* **PRIN***'s cigarette glowing in the dark.* **PRIN** *gets up out of a chaise and walks into the light. She carries a cigarette and a tumbler full of amber booze.)*

PRIN. I love this time of night. My mother would give me beer sometimes. In my bottle.

FRAN. No shit?

PRIN. When I cried too much.

FRAN. That's funny 'cause you don't like beer now.

PRIN. Ah, that's kid stuff. You and Con settle in okay?

FRAN. Oh yeah. Yeah. Real nice.

PRIN. So, how you been since the playoffs?

FRAN. Oh you know. Pretty good. I'm tired, is all. Tired of being tired, too.

PRIN. The little bruiser keeps you busy, huh?

FRAN. Yeah, he does. But I wouldn't trade it, Prin. He can catch a hardball now, I told you that right?

PRIN. Thought he liked tennis.

FRAN. He does. I'm trying to discourage him. Like you said, who watches tennis?

PRIN. That's the spirit. If he has a shot at really doing anything, team sports, dude.

FRAN. So, how you been?

PRIN. Pretty good, pretty fucking good.

FRAN. Yeah, sounds like business is going great.

PRIN. Business is always just business at the end of the day. After a certain point, how much shit can you buy with all the money you make. There's more important things in life.

FRAN. Who are you? What have you done with my friend Prin?

PRIN. Can I show you something, Fran?

FRAN. Am I going to have to show you mine, too?

PRIN. No, no. Hold my cig.

> (**FRAN** *takes* **PRIN***'s cigarette and takes a drag off of it while* **PRIN** *fishes in her pocket. She pulls out a small jewelry box and opens it.*)

FRAN. Wow, that is nice. Really nice. Terri's gonna love it. Con and I...I hope Terri likes what we got her. We took a bit of a risk.

PRIN. Got one for myself, too.

FRAN. Oh.

> *(then, getting it)*

Oh...Prin. Does that mean what I think means?

PRIN. I'm giving it to her, man. To Terri.

FRAN. Are you shitting me?

PRIN. If the pope falls in the woods, does he make a sound?

FRAN. Are you having a wedding? This is blowing my mind.

PRIN. No wedding. No public thing. Just – I just – I love her.

FRAN. You always love 'em, pal.

PRIN. No, I don' think so. I don't think I really knew what that meant before.

FRAN. When did you decide this?

PRIN. I started thinking about it when her mom got sick. You know, I wondered if I could hack it. I just loved her more. I didn't expect that. I figured, if I can get through this and still be crazy about her, then maybe it's time to make it official.

FRAN. Wow, that is great. That is fucking great.

PRIN. Think she'll have me?

FRAN. Oh, god. Totally.

PRIN. I'm giving it to her Sunday night, at dinner. I'm going to be an old married lady, just like you.

FRAN. Ugh. God, I hope not.

PRIN. Rough night, huh?

FRAN. Huh?

PRIN. Come on, Fran, something's up. You've got that twitch under your eye.

FRAN. I don't know.

PRIN. I told you my secret. It *is* a secret, by the way. No telling anyone. Not even Con.

FRAN. Con's pissed at me, I guess.

PRIN. Okay. Have a schnort.

(FRAN's hand shakes as she pours herself a shot.)

You're fucking shaking like a leaf.

FRAN. It's totally fucked up.

PRIN. Sit back. Here's a smoke.

(She hands FRAN a lit cigarette.)

Now, speak, my friend. What's up?

FRAN. Oh, man. Well, aside from Con threatening to break up with me, nothing much.

PRIN. So, Con is upset.

FRAN. Fuck yeah, she is. Oh, man, Prin. It's intense. I don't know how to say this. She says if we don't have sex by this weekend...she's going to...well, she didn't say exactly. But the implication was that she's going to leave me? Is that possible?

PRIN. Just give her some time to cool off. She'll be sweet as can be tomorrow. Hell, make-up sex is the best anyway.

FRAN. That's kind of the problem. She wants to have sex, you know? But I don't feel like it.

PRIN. I don't understand.

FRAN. I'm serious. I mean, being pregnant was weird, I've got hormones now and shit and I'm all –

PRIN. Easy, Fran. Everybody goes through these dry spells, even me.

FRAN. *(incredulous)* Yeah?

PRIN. Yeah. That year I was having the change of life. Sometimes I'd go weeks. I just couldn't think about it.

FRAN. *(despondent)* Weeks.

PRIN. How long's it been for you and Con?

FRAN. Four years.

PRIN. Holy Mother of God. I'd be dead.

FRAN. It's my fault. Con wants to.

PRIN. How come you didn't talk to me about this?

FRAN. I don't know.

PRIN. Man, if you told me sooner, we could have figured something out. Four years. Jesus Christ.

FRAN. What am I going to do?

PRIN. Well, what's the deal? You love her, right?

FRAN. More than anything. Except Basil.

PRIN. But you don't want to fuck her?

FRAN. I don't want to fuck anything right now. And then there's all this pressure.

PRIN. I think Con's right. I think you've got to fuck her.

FRAN. When I don't feel like it?

PRIN. You gotta prime the pump when it's dry.

FRAN. Oh, okay. I guess.

PRIN. Who knows you better than me?

FRAN. Nobody.

PRIN. You and Con are going to be fine.

Courtyard, Saturday Afternoon

(*JONI sits facing an easel. We watch her blind face as she dips her fingers in to pots of paint and decorates a ceramic roof tile.*)

JONI. What we're talking about here is 'predetermination'. Fate. The belief that one's destiny is sealed from the moment we're born. There's nothing we can do to change it.

(*then*)

No. Thomas Aquinas is "order of determination." That's different.

(*The Main Gate opens.*)

Oh shit. I gotta go.

(*JONI removes the ear-bud of her cell phone and starts cleaning up.*)

(*TERRI and CON enter, carrying large outlet shopping bags.*)

TERRI. I'm serious, Con. They're gorgeous on you!

CON. You don't think forty-four is a little old for low-riders?

TERRI. Honey, not your forty-four.

CON. Really?

TERRI. Hot! Very hot!

CON. Oh you! I'm gonna go change. Meet me back at the pool.

(*CON goes into her casita.*)

(*The front gate opens. PRIN and FRAN enter carrying their golf bags.*)

FRAN. I don't know what it is. My swing is just fucking gone.

PRIN. I'm telling you, Franski, we're going out again and I'm giving you a Bloody Mary to prove my theory.

TERRI. Hey! How was golf?

PRIN. Great.

(FRAN plops down on a chaise, exhausted.)

FRAN. Hot!

TERRI. You two missed a great time at the outlets.

(FRAN and PRIN exchange looks.)

Con and I had a blast. She got the hottest pair of jeans, Fran. You should check them out.

FRAN. I will. Definitely.

(FRAN doesn't move.)

TERRI. *(sympathetically)* You tired, Fran?

FRAN. Pooped.

(TERRI kicks off her sandals and begins to undress completely.)

TERRI. The sun is really hot. I can't believe this whole 'no nudity' thing. It's so stupid.

JONI. I don't make the rules.

(Startled, TERRI zips up.)

TERRI. Oh, Joni. I didn't see you there.

JONI. I didn't see you, either.

TERRI. What? Oh, ha ha.

PRIN. Hey, Joni, what are you painting?

(PRIN walks over and looks at JONI's painting.)

PRIN. Looks like someone's been messing with your paint pots.

JONI. If so, then it was meant to be.

TERRI. Honey. How about a swim?

(The painted tile grabs TERRI's attention.)

TERRI. Wow. That's so…powerful.

PRIN. Is that a potato?

TERRI. I think it's a baby. Right?

JONI. I just paint what I see.

TERRI. I don't know why, but…it so moves me.

JONI. You should take it.

TERRI. Oh, no. I couldn't. I mean, I would have to pay you for it.

PRIN. Whatever you like, baby.

(then)

What's the asking price, Joni?

JONI. No, no. I insist. A belated birthday present.

TERRI. My birthday's not till tomorrow.

JONI. Of course. I meant to say 'early'.

TERRI. Really? I don't know what to say.

(JONI hands TERRI the tile. More than bad art passes between them.)

(TERRI gives JONI a quick hug and takes the painted tile.)

I'm taking it before you change your mind.

(TERRI exits to their casita to hang up her new piece of art.)

(PRIN sits on a chaise, lights up a cigarette and smokes.)

PRIN. You just made my girl very happy.

JONI. Pleasure is fleeting. All life is suffering, the Buddha says.

(Her cell phone rings. JONI puts her ear-bud in and answers, nonchalantly.)

Casitas Bonitas. Speak.

(PRIN watches JONI go into the office, then takes off her shoes and puts her feet in the water.)

Prin and Terri's Casita

(TERRI *has hung the painted roof tile on the wall behind the bed.*)

(*The ugly painting is a madonna and child portrait in bizarre relief, almost like a negative of a painting.* PRIN *is right—the child does look like a potato.*)

(TERRI *stares at it while she strips down to her bikini.*)

Courtyard

FRAN. God, it's hot.

PRIN. Go inside with your girl. Take a "nap."

FRAN. A nap. That sounds great.

(**FRAN** *goes into her casita.*)

Con and Fran's Casita

(**CON** *is trying on her new low-riders.* **FRAN** *enters.*)

FRAN. Hey! How was the outlets?

CON. Fine.

FRAN. Those your new jeans?

CON. Yep.

FRAN. I like them. They're cute.

CON. Really?

FRAN. Yeah. Turn around.

(**CON** *spins.*)

Nice. Is your crack supposed to be hanging out like that?

(**CON** *slams the bathroom door.*)

(**FRAN** *flops down on the bed.*)

Courtyard

(TERRI *enters the courtyard, climbs on top of* PRIN *and kisses her.*)

TERRI. Where's Fran?

PRIN. Inside.

TERRI. Oh, that's good.

(PRIN *and* TERRI *kiss.* PRIN *nuzzles* TERRI*'s neck.*)

PRIN. This little spot right here is one thing I could not live without.

TERRI. That's right.

(CON *enters the courtyard, now wearing her swimsuit, book in hand. She watches* PRIN *and* TERRI, *who don't see her.*)

PRIN. And no matter who else loves you, this will always be mine.

TERRI. No one is ever gonna love me like you.

PRIN. Behind the ear will always be mine.

(CON *takes a deep frustrated sigh. Stay or go? She considers going back into her casita, both options look equally unpleasant.*)

(TERRI *sees* CON *and sits up.*)

TERRI. Oh…hi, Con.

CON. Hi.

TERRI. Did Fran see your new jeans?

CON. Yep.

TERRI. What'd she say?

CON. Nothing that I can repeat in mixed company.

TERRI. See? I told you they were hot.

(PRIN *laughs.*)

PRIN. Two o'clock. Time to rev up the blender.

TERRI. Sounds great, babe.

(PRIN *exits.*)

TERRI. Is that the new *Harry Potter?*

CON. Yep.

TERRI. The sun feels great, doesn't it?

CON. Hot.

TERRI. You should definitely go back and get those shoes at Cole Haan.

CON. Mm-hm.

TERRI. You're not mad at me, are you?

CON. No. Why would I be mad at you?

TERRI. Oh, the last six months have been so shitty. I know I haven't been a very good friend lately.

CON. Please, with all you're going through.

TERRI. And you've been so good to me. All those late-night phone calls about my mom and my adoption and my search. I must drive you crazy.

CON. Terri, you're my friend.

TERRI. I've missed you and Basil so much.

CON. Well, you have come over more. He misses you, too. He's getting so big you won't recognize him.

TERRI. I should. Hey, you never finished telling me about that meeting.

CON. Same as always. The city keeps threatening to close the hospital down and we keep fighting like hell to keep it open.

TERRI. You help so many people.

CON. Doctors help people. Administrators exasperate them.

TERRI. And you and Fran?

CON. We're good.

TERRI. Are you two still in counseling?

CON. Yep.

TERRI. How's that going?

CON. Good.

TERRI. So things are good?

CON. Things are good.

(PRIN *re-enters with drinks.*)

PRIN. Drinks are on.

(PRIN *pours one for* TERRI.)

TERRI. Mmm. Icy cold. Delicious.

PRIN. Sure I can't help you out, Con?

CON. I'm staying hydrated.

PRIN. Smart lady.

(PRIN *gets in the pool with her drink.* CON *goes back to her book.*)

TERRI. *(to* PRIN*)* How's the water?

PRIN. It's perfection.

TERRI. Con? Want to go in?

CON. I don't feel like getting wet.

(TERRI *gets into the pool.*)

PRIN. God, this jet of water feels good on my back.

(TERRI *crosses to* PRIN. *She puts her drink down next to* PRIN*'s and kisses her.*)

TERRI. And how does this feel?

(*We can't see what* TERRI *is doing to* PRIN *under the water, but from the look on* PRIN*'s face, it's pretty damn good.*)

PRIN. Mmm. Nice.

(CON *drops her book a little and watches them while they make out. After a moment, they stop kissing.*)

I think we better take this inside.

(TERRI *dunks under the water then walks out of the pool.*)

(CON*'s eyes follow* TERRI*'s dripping wet body as she disappears into the casita.*)

(PRIN *carries their drinks inside and closes the door behind her.*)

(**CON** *sits there. No longer able to read her book. She looks at the margarita pitcher, longingly.*)

(*She looks around then takes a long gulp out of the pitcher.*)

(*She goes into the pool and stands where* **PRIN** *was, using the pool jet to massage her own lower back.*)

(*After a moment, she turns around, the jet now massaging a totally different "muscle." She writhes in pleasure. Then orgasms.*)

Courtyard, Saturday Night

(PRIN enters. She hums, carrying a plate of steaks. She knocks on FRAN and CON's door. She's in a totally jovial mood.)

PRIN. Awake! The hour of barbecuing is upon us.

(She goes into her own casita, where TERRI sleeps on the bed.)

(to TERRI) Hey, sleepy head.

TERRI. *(sleepy)* But I'm having such a nice nap.

PRIN. And now you're going to have a nice dinner. Come on. Do I have to come in there and get you?

TERRI. Yes.

PRIN. No. Enough of that for now.

TERRI. Okay, coming.

PRIN. *(knocking again on FRAN and CON's door.)* Ladies! Rise and shine!

(FRAN comes stumbling out, totally groggy.)

FRAN. Hey.

PRIN. Well, hello, Casanova. How'd it go in there?

FRAN. I think I could sleep 'round the clock.

PRIN. Sexy. Very sexy. Where's Con?

FRAN. *(realizing she's not there)* I don't know.

(CON enters from the main gate in an overly cheery mood carrying a couple of small bags.)

CON. Hello!

PRIN. Hey, where've ya been?

CON. Oh! I went for a walk. Hot but nice.

FRAN. Hey, honey.

CON. Hey.

FRAN. Did you walk downtown?

CON. Yep.

(TERRI enters the courtyard.)

TERRI. Hey, everybody.

CON. Hey, Terri. That skirt looks great.

TERRI. Thanks.

(**PRIN** *feels her up.*)

FRAN. I thought we were going to walk downtown later.

CON. You wanted to sleep. I let you sleep. What's up with your hair?

FRAN. I don't know. What?

CON. You've got Bozo hair. Would you go fix it, please?

(**FRAN** *messes with her hair, only making matters worse.*)

CON. Go inside and look at what you're doing.

FRAN. I just sat down.

CON. Okay, sit there like that then.

(**FRAN** *drags herself up and into the casita.*)

TERRI. Honey, what can we do?

CON. Yeah. How can we help, Prin?

PRIN. Just sit there and look sexy.

CON. I'll do what I can.

PRIN. That will be more than enough.

CON. Ha.

PRIN. Margaritas, ladies?

TERRI. Sure.

(*taking in the atmosphere*)

Oh, it's going to be a beautiful night. It's going to cool all the way down to 90.

PRIN. (*offering her a margarita*) Con? Can I interest you?

(**FRAN** *enters wearing a baseball cap over her Bozo hair – OR – hair completely wet down and parted in the middle.*)

FRAN. How's this? Better?

CON. (*looks at* **FRAN** *and then back at the margarita pitcher*) You know what? Yes, give me a margarita.

PRIN. *(handing her a drink)* Your wish is my command.

CON. Thank you.

(sips)

Hoo! I'd forgotten how strong your drinks are!

PRIN. Strong, like bull!

FRAN. Oh. Are we drinking?

CON. I'm having a drink.

FRAN. Does that mean it's okay if I have one?

CON. Well, that's up to you, isn't it? What do you want, a permission slip?

FRAN. *(totally confused)* Well –

PRIN. Oh, for fuck's sake, Fran.

(**PRIN** *pours her a drink.*)

Alright. Now that we all have a beverage, I'd like to propose a toast. To Terri on her 37th birthday!

ALL. To Terri.

TERRI. Thank you. I feel very happy right now. I haven't felt this way in a while. Thanks, you guys, for being here.

(She gives **PRIN** *a kiss.)*

Thank you, baby.

PRIN. You're welcome. Okay. How do people want their steaks?

TERRI. Medium.

CON. Medium rare.

(**PRIN** *puts an apron on* **FRAN** *and hands her a barbecue fork.*)

PRIN. And you know I want mine bloody. I'm counting on you pal. The success of this barbeque is all going to come down to Francesa Cancellaro, maestro of the grill.

FRAN. You've prepared them with the Dr. Pepper marinade?

PRIN. You know it.

FRAN. Then sit back and relax. The maestro is in!

PRIN. Beautiful!

TERRI. You're so silly.

PRIN. Life's too short to be serious!

CON. She's just excited about your present, Terri.

TERRI. What present?

PRIN. Fran?

FRAN. Huh?

CON. Oh, she told me this morning.

TERRI. What is it?

PRIN. I said don't tell anybody!

FRAN. Anybody! Con's not anybody.

TERRI. Prin, what have you done? You didn't buy me a boat, did you? You guys, please tell me she didn't buy a boat.

CON. No, it's not a boat.

TERRI. Because I don't want a boat, Prin. If you want to buy one for yourself go ahead but I don't need a boat.

CON. *(pointedly)* It's really quite amazing what she got you.

FRAN. Con got you an amazing present, Terri. Really. Amazing.

CON. Fran! Shh!

FRAN. What?

> *(CON sighs impatiently.)*

TERRI. It's okay, you guys.

PRIN. Not another one of Con's "original" gifts.

CON. What? I don't like generic gifts.

PRIN. I'll say. I love my "dubloons"

CON. You know what, Prin?

PRIN. "Authentic pirate treasure."

CON. Next year I'm getting you gift soaps.

PRIN. Ahoy, matey. That's an original gift!

CON. I'm getting you scented candles from now on. Or a picture frame. You'd like that.

FRAN. Oh yeah, scented candles. She'd love that.

CON. Worse yet, I'll send Fran out to get your present.

FRAN. Hey.

CON. What? I'm joking. It's a joke.

TERRI. Hey, have you talked to Fran's mom? How's B doing?

CON. He's having the time of his life. He's on the sugar cereal and dairy diet. Maria can't say no to him. It's going to take us months to undo the damage.

FRAN. You were the one who wanted to leave him.

CON. What?

FRAN. I'm just saying.

CON. What were we going to do? Leave him in the car? They don't take kids here, Fran. This is a lesbian resort. Where you come to...be lesbians. I miss him too.

FRAN. I know that.

CON. No, I know. Those two have their special thing.

TERRI. What do you mean?

CON. Terri, you know how they are. Melded. A unit. They have this mystical connection. It's beautiful.

PRIN. Kind of like us, babe.

CON. No, Prin, not like you.

TERRI. Fran, do you think that's true?

FRAN. I don't know.

CON. Oh, come on, Fran. You say to me, "I feel like he's – me. It's like his shit is my shit. When he pukes it's the same as my puke."

PRIN. Yeah, you're right. Not like us.

FRAN. Did we need to share that?

CON. It's biology. You can't get around it. You and Basil just have this...thing between you.

FRAN. You and Basil have a thing.

CON. Of course we do. He's my guy. That's not my point, Fran.

TERRI. Hey, are we all doing okay here?

CON. Yeah. We're great.

PRIN. How about a little dividend?

CON & FRAN. Yes. Definitely.

(**PRIN** *refills* **FRAN** *and* **CON** *'s glasses.*)

TERRI. Oh, you guys. Don't stress. It's all going to be okay.

CON. What are we even talking about?

TERRI. It's your first time alone in a long time. It's not surprising if you're a little...out of sync.

CON. We're in sync. We're fine.

(*then*)

Fran, do you need to pump?

FRAN. I'm okay.

CON. I don't know if you guys have noticed. But underneath those baggy polo shirts she wears her tits are amazing.

FRAN. Con.

CON. What? And the milk is incredible. The taste of it is really surprising – like a combination of pineapple and love. Pure love.

FRAN. I think she's getting a little drunk.

TERRI. You've tasted her milk?

CON. When I bottle feed him. Ingrid, our doula, said it was a way for me to feel more a part of the process.

PRIN. Weird.

CON. Weird. Right, Prin. You wouldn't know a mothering instinct if it hit you in the face.

PRIN. True. I can't recall a mothering instinct hitting me in the face, although my mother did on many occasions.

TERRI. Oh, honey.

PRIN. What? It's the truth.

TERRI. I know. But it's so brutal.

PRIN. It was brutal, Kitten. She was mean. I'm just stating a fact. Motherhood is overrated in my opinion.

FRAN. I just hope I can be a good mom to the kid.

TERRI. You're a great mom, Fran.

FRAN. I've never loved anyone the way I love him.

CON. Oh yes, totally. It's like this instinctual thing that happens where you would just die for him, you would kill for him.

PRIN. I think that's just love.

CON. A very particular kind of love.

PRIN. I feel that way about Terri.

TERRI. You do?

CON. You would tear someone's jugular out with your teeth for Terri? Because that's the kind of feeling I'm talking about.

FRAN. Well, I don't know if I could do that.

CON. Do you have to disagree with everything I say?

FRAN. Well, yeah, when it's something ridiculous like that.

CON. You just have to agree with whatever Prin says.

FRAN. No, I just don't think we're like wolves.

CON. I didn't say wolves. How did you get that out of what I said? Jesus!

PRIN. So. You two have sex yet?

CON. What?

PRIN. If you went at each other in bed the way you're going at each other right now, you wouldn't have any problems.

CON. What?

PRIN. Listen, Con. I'm on *your* side. If I went without sex for four years I'd be a way bigger bitch than you.

CON. *(to FRAN)* Tell me you didn't do what I think you did.

TERRI. *(to PRIN)* Honey. That's just not helpful.

PRIN. I told Fran straight out –

CON. Fran, how could you?

TERRI. Fran just needs to talk.

PRIN. Fran just needs to fuck you.

CON. Unbelievable!

PRIN. But true!

CON. I can't believe you told them, when I specifically asked you not to.

FRAN. It fell out.

CON. What's your damage, Fran. Is nothing private?

PRIN. Give her a break, Con. You scared the shit out of her.

CON. I will not allow you to gang up on me.

PRIN. It's only because you're so formidable.

CON. This topic is not up for discussion.

TERRI. Maybe talking about it will help.

CON. Don't psychoanalyze me, Terri.

PRIN. That's what I said, Con. The time for talk is over.

CON. Excuse me, Prin, if I don't want to take relationship advice from someone who thinks a lap dance is intimacy.

PRIN. Have you ever had a lap dance?

CON. You think you've got it all figured out now, as usual. Well, I will believe it when I see it.

PRIN. Watch and learn, Con.

CON. Learn from you? Based on your illustrious track record the best thing for me to do right now is to dump Fran, find some other woman, run off with her and start all over again.

FRAN. Hon –

CON. What? Are you going to tell me that's not true? I believe you were the one who dubbed your friend Prin "The Master of Escape."

FRAN. Con. Don't go there.

CON. First, you used, what was her name? Charlotte, to escape from Michigan.

PRIN. We were talking about your sex life. But keep going, Con, this is good.

CON. Then there was Ellie. She lasted a year. When she wanted to move in with you, you took off to Europe. Andrea fell in love with you. How'd you get out of that one? Oh yeah. You went bankrupt!

FRAN. That's absurd.

CON. She was back in business two weeks later, without so much as a hiccup.

FRAN. Yeah, okay.

CON. Then there was Nicole. Then there was Dierdre.

TERRI. That's enough.

CON. No, you're right. If I included all the one-night stands and mistresses we'd be here all night. I actually thought you had something with Carol. Who we loved. But of course you had to go and dump her when you met…

TERRI. …me!

PRIN. I was just working my way up to the right girl.

CON. I was just trying to point out a pattern.

(JONI *enters the courtyard without anyone noticing and quietly cleans up.*)

PRIN. That's all well and good, Con, but I'm not your problem.

CON. I wish somebody could tell us what our problem is.

TERRI. You two just need more time alone.

CON. This is it. This is our time. We're wasting it.

FRAN. The weekend's not over.

CON. What's going to change, Fran? You have zero interest in me, in sex, in ever having sex again.

FRAN. Honey, I'm just exhausted.

CON. I'm exhausted, too.

TERRI. Have you two tried different things? Like, I don't know…like sensual massage.

CON & FRAN. Yes.

TERRI. Role playing?

CON & FRAN. Yes.

TERRI. Have you tried porn?

CON. Tried it? I don't know if there's any left we haven't tried.

FRAN. *You* haven't tried.

CON. I like erotica. So what?

PRIN. Penthouse letters. Very hifalutin.

CON. Terri, we've done every exercise in the book. Nothing makes you feel less sexy than trying to make love "paint-by-numbers" style.

FRAN. I'm so glad you said that. I thought it was only me.

CON. Those exercises are bullshit!

JONI. It all comes down to the phantom penis.

PRIN. Joni's right. If you want to keep it going you've got to have some butch/femme sustaining energy.

FRAN. What?

CON. We've used dildos…

PRIN. It's not the dick, it's the attitude. That's what's missing. You need a little testosterone in the relationship. The yin and the yang.

CON. We've never had testosterone in our relationship.

PRIN. Not true. Fran wasn't always such a femme.

FRAN. Who're you calling a femme?

TERRI. What's wrong with being a femme?

FRAN. Nothing, except I'm not one.

CON. I don't believe in butch and femme.

PRIN. No wonder you're up shit's creek.

CON. What's the point of being a lesbian if you're just aping some heterosexual paradigm?

PRIN. It's the attitude, I'm telling you. You want Fran to take you like a caveman.

CON. Unlike you, Prin, I've had sex with actual men, and I had enough to know that is not what I want.

PRIN. Your 1970's politically-correct-no-penetration-bullshit is just a fast track to lesbian bed death.

CON. So according to you the ghost penis or whatever you call it is the only way to keep the spark.

TERRI. I don't think we ever had a spark, really.

FRAN. What, are you kidding?

TERRI. It's more like a slow burn. We just – know each other somehow. We just read each other. Right, honey?

PRIN. Something like that.

CON. That's beautiful. It'd be a lot harder to maintain, though, if you had a kid sleeping between you.

FRAN. Sideways.

CON. Sideways.

TERRI. Well sure.

PRIN. I told you that kid was gonna fuck everything up.

CON. Before the baby, I used to have to fight Fran off.

FRAN. As I recall, you didn't fight all that hard.

PRIN. As I recall, you two were arrested in La Jolla for public indecency.

CON. Gone are the days, my friend…

TERRI. But you're happy you had Basil.

FRAN. Oh yeah.

CON. Totally.

TERRI. *(priming the pump)* I mean think about your lives with him. Isn't it worth all the hard parts? Remember when he was born?

FRAN. Remember? I remember thinking somebody please kill me right now and put me out of my misery.

CON. Well, you did it without anesthesia.

TERRI. Oh, tell that story!

FRAN. Oh, haven't you heard that story a million times?

PRIN. A million and one.

TERRI. Oh, tell it for me. For my birthday.

(FRAN looks to CON, who is still sulking. FRAN launches anyway. She is a bad story teller.)

FRAN. So, I was holding onto the shopping cart, and the contractions started coming, and Con was ignoring me –

CON. I was not ignoring you.

FRAN. This one contraction came and it was really painful, and I was screaming, and Con was, like, doot-de-doo, where's the jumbo-sized toilet paper?

CON. She was screaming, but she wasn't making any noise.

FRAN. Yeah, I was like –

(FRAN *does a breathy, voiceless scream.*)

CON. So I didn't hear her.

FRAN. And I was like, "Con? Con? Con? Con? Con?"

CON. So I noticed she was gone and I turned around and she was holding onto the shopping cart, and she was, she looked terrible. She was white as a ghost. My heart stopped and I was like, "I'm going to get the car."

FRAN. And I was like, "Honey, the baby…" And she was like…

CON. I was like, "Honey, you're having a contraction. Hang on, I'm gonna get the car." So I'm running to the car and I'm looking for my keys in my purse and I can't find them and trying to rush and all like, "Shit, shit, shit," and then I heard this screaming. All these young men were screaming and I turned and there was Fran on her hands and knees in a huge puddle and I nearly passed out and…

FRAN. You! Those stock boys will never recover.

CON. And I was like, "Honey, your water broke!"

FRAN. And I was like, "No! No! The baby!"

CON. And I was freaking out. I thought something terrible had happened. I said, "The baby's fine." And she said…

FRAN. I said, "The baby is out! There's a baby in my sweatpants."

CON. I thought she was hallucinating. But then I saw this big bulge.

PRIN. Is that a baby in your pants or are you just happy to see me?

CON. And it was Basil. And somebody called an ambulance. And we just sat there in aisle four of the Costco holding Basil and crying.

FRAN. Con held him. I was afraid to touch him. I wanted to make sure we were doing the right thing. I wanted to leave him in my pants until the ambulance came but Con said… oh, I'll never forget. She said, "Of course we can hold him. He's our son. We can hold him forever."

(then)

God, he came fast. I'll say that for him.

CON. Basil loves hearing that story.

PRIN. Because it puts him to sleep?

FRAN. *(affectionately)* Shut up.

(TERRI has teared up.)

TERRI. I love it. So beautiful. I always wished Betty could tell me my birth story. You guys are so blessed.

FRAN. He *is* a cute kid.

CON. Yeah. He is.

(CON starts to cry.)

TERRI. Honey?

CON. What's wrong with me?

FRAN. Nothing!

CON. I am so tired of having to be the bitch!

TERRI. Oh, honey.

CON. I know you guys are trying to help and I know you care about us, but it is so different with a kid.

TERRI. It's an awesome responsibility.

CON. And Fran, forgive me, is just out to lunch sometimes.

FRAN. It's easier to be out to lunch. You should try being out to lunch sometimes.

CON. Yeah, maybe I should.

FRAN. And I'll try being the bitch.

CON. *(laughs)* Yeah, right.

TERRI. I don't think you have it in you, Franny.

FRAN. I could surprise you all.

CON. Oh, god. What a night.

PRIN. Feel better?

CON. I feel drunk is what I feel!

FRAN. I feel not drunk enough! Fill 'er up, Dr. Cuervo!

> (*PRIN starts refilling glasses.*)

JONI. Fire.

> (*They all look at her, perplexed.*)
>
> Fire.
>
> (*Then…*)

CON. The steaks! Prin, the steaks!

> (*CON jumps up. FRAN falls.*)

FRAN. Whoa, I'm drunk!

> (*TERRI and CON help FRAN up, while PRIN rushes to the smoking grill and opens it.*)

PRIN. Steaks well done.

TERRI. Oh no!

CON. All that expensive meat!

FRAN. Shit! I fucked up!

CON. No you didn't, honey.

PRIN. No, no! No problemo. Just think of it as a sacrifice to the gods. Now, if you'll excuse me, I think I'll retire to the "blendatorium" to see what I can improvise.

> (*PRIN grabs blender and exits.*)

TERRI. Wow. This is a lot of booze with no food.

CON. I know. It's kinda good, isn't it?

TERRI. Con. You are adorable when you're drunk.

CON. Really? You don't think I'm just mean?

TERRI. Never.

CON. Oh, Terri, we love you. Fran, come over here and tell Terri how much we love her.

FRAN. We fucking love you, Terri.

TERRI. I love you, too.

CON. We all love each other so much!

(**PRIN** *re-enters carrying a bag of corn chips, a container and a bottle of tequila.*)

PRIN. Corn chips and fat-free sour cream. 'S all I got.

CON. What happened to corn on the cob?

PRIN. Never made it to the grill. We got plenty more tequila, though.

(**FRAN** *pours herself a shot. Drinks it. They start eating the chips.*)

CON. God, I am so much hungrier than I realized.

FRAN. *(nibbling on **CON**'s arm)* I'm just going to snack on this.

CON. What's gotten into you?

FRAN. I don't know. I think it might be a little…

*(whispering into **CON**'s ear)*

…tequila.

CON. Tequila, that must be it. I haven't felt this relaxed in months.

FRAN. Years.

CON. All that therapy, who knew we just needed tequila?

PRIN. I did!

(**PRIN** *pours **CON** a shot.*)

(**CON** *downs the shot.*)

CON. Of course you did. This reminds me of college.

TERRI. What do you mean?

CON. How many shots it'd take for me to fake heterosexual feelings.

TERRI. Was it a lot?

CON. Honey, I'd have to drink a whole bottle before you could get me to eat the worm, if you know what I mean.

FRAN. I think under the right circumstances I could be with a guy.

CON. Oh, here we go.

TERRI. You, really?

CON. She fucks one gay guy in 1981 because she's tripping on Ecstacy and she thinks she's bi.

FRAN. I don't believe in labels.

TERRI. I never tried it but I don't think I'd like it.

CON. Prin is man enough for you.

PRIN. Terri's our only virgin.

CON. *(to PRIN)* Well, besides you.

(laughing)

The uber-homosexual.

FRAN. *(going back to her story)* I wonder whatever happened to that guy. What was his name?

PRIN. I am not a virgin.

CON. Huh?

PRIN. I am not a virgin.

CON. Am I super drunk or did you just say you fucked a guy?

PRIN. It depends what you mean by "fucked."

CON. Okay, President Clinton, what the hell are you talking about?

TERRI. You never told me about this.

FRAN. You never told *me* about this.

PRIN. What's to tell? I was young, I was stupid, he had a hot girlfriend.

FRAN. Ugh, now I've got that picture in my mind.

PRIN. It was just a dick. What's the big deal?

CON. Me, Fran, Terri fucking a guy, no big deal. You? Big deal.

TERRI. It only makes me love you more.

PRIN. Yeh. I gotta pee.

(PRIN exits to the Casita.)

CON. Well, now my mind is officially blown.

FRAN. You think you know someone.

CON. Well, if Prin can fuck a guy, maybe we can have sex this weekend.

FRAN. Kinda makes you believe in the impossible.

(CON *and* FRAN *kiss.*)

TERRI. Here's to Con and Fran. May the magic of the desert stars shine on them tonight.

CON. To Con and Fran!

(JONI *starts drumming.*)

(*The three of them watch her, mystified for a moment. Then...*)

Hey, Joni, read our keys.

FRAN. Yeah!

(JONI *continues drumming.*)

JONI. Now is not an auspicious time.

CON. Come on. Fran and I are treating Terri for her birthday.

(JONI *puts down her drum. She ritually bows to it and quietly says...*)

JONI. Scraboo.

(CON *guides* JONI *to a chair at the table.*)

TERRI. Guys. You don't have to do this.

FRAN. Yeah, we do!

CON. How does it work?

JONI. First. Toss the keys on to the table.

TERRI. I don't have any keys.

FRAN. Can she use mine?

TERRI. I doubt it.

JONI. Yes.

(FRAN *hands* TERRI *her keys.*)

TERRI. Okay, but only good news. It's my birthday!

CON. I'll throw in an extra ten bucks if you don't tell her any bad news.

JONI. It is the keys that speak, not I.

TERRI. I just toss them?

(JONI *nods.*)

CON. Does she rub them or anything?

JONI. No.

(TERRI *tosses the keys. All gather around while* JONI *feels the keys.*)

(PRIN *enters.*)

PRIN. Why'd it get so deadly quiet around here?

CON. Joni's giving Terri a key reading.

(PRIN *goes to* TERRI*'s side.*)

JONI. Aaahhh... The house key. Your heart key. It points toward the north. The north is orientation, the guiding star.

FRAN. Who knew?

CON. Shhh!

JONI. Your house key is sideways which can mean ambivalence or doubt. Most likely, you are a soul still searching for a home – your true home.

(PRIN *puts an arm around* TERRI*'s shoulder.*)

PRIN. Not for long...

JONI. This key is travel.

FRAN. *(proudly)* The Saab.

JONI. Your toss left the key pointing straight up.

FRAN. That sounds like a good sign.

JONI. It means you have a rough journey ahead.

(FRAN *laughs at the irony. But* TERRI *is quiet, taking this seriously.*)

Is this...

FRAN. The mailbox key.

JONI. The key of letters – the messenger key. You will receive something in writing. Something that will transform you.

(CON gasps.)

JONI. This key is a lock. A mystery.

FRAN. That's the key to my locker at the club.

JONI. The lock key is crossed with the heart key. You are puzzling over something? You have a question...about your mother. Is there something you want to ask?

(after a long silence)

TERRI. She knew how much I loved her, right?

JONI. No.

TERRI. No?

JONI. Your mother is coming closer to you.

TERRI. Are you talking about my birth mother?

JONI. Traveling very fast.

CON. Oh my god. Oh my god.

JONI. You cannot change what has been set in motion.

TERRI. I haven't set anything in motion.

CON. I'm no psychic but this makes so much sense.

TERRI. It does?

CON. Trust me! All will be revealed.

(to FRAN)

On your birthday...

FRAN. Shush, shush, shush.

(FRAN and CON are amazed.)

PRIN. This is a little oogly-boogly for me.

(PRIN abandons TERRI's side, takes her drink and gets in the pool.)

TERRI. What do you mean my mother's coming closer?

JONI. If you are squeamish, don't prod the beach rubble.

(JONI stands up and downs a margarita.)

That's all I got. No glass by the pool, please. 'Night, ladies.

(JONI shuffles off, exhausted.)

FRAN. That was freaky!

CON. Intense, right? Did it make the hair stand up on the back of your neck?

(CON *feels* FRAN *up.*)

FRAN. God, that feels good.

PRIN. Come on in, girls. The water's fine.

FRAN. Yes! Let's go swimming.

CON. That sounds delicious.

PRIN. I want to see some wet lesbians.

(FRAN *and* CON *grab their drinks and ease into the pool.*)

FRAN. *(reacting to the water)* Eee!

CON. I can see by your erect nipples which point towards the east that the water is cold tonight. Scraboo.

FRAN. No, it's great. Ah!

(CON *peels off her wrap.*)

Woo woo, baby.

(CON *does a little dance and gets into the pool, holding her drink. She walks over to* FRAN *and gives her a big, sloppy kiss.*)

(TERRI *quietly starts cleaning up.*)

CON. Oh, man! This is so nice! I wish I could be naked.

PRIN. Go for it.

CON. Remember what happened last time? Jorel almost forbade me from ever returning.

PRIN. Fuck her. She's in Guatamala.

CON. Yeah, but I don't trust that Joni. She'll fucking call them.

FRAN. *(shushing her)* Sh! Sh! Sh!

(CON *jumps on* FRAN. *They wrestle playfully.*)

CON. No fair! I can't take off your bra, you'd flood the pool.

PRIN. Ter, hand me the booze, will ya.

(**TERRI** *hands* **PRINCESS** *the bottle of tequila.*)

TERRI. You guys better take it easy.

FRAN. Why? No kid, no work. Shit. We should've done this a year ago.

(*She takes the bottle from* **PRIN** *and swigs.*)

PRIN. *(to* **TERRI***)* Baby, come in.

TERRI. I don't know.

FRAN. What do the keys say?

CON. Magic 8 ball, will I get laid tonight?

TERRI. I think I'm going to go inside.

PRIN. No.

TERRI. That reading kind of got to me. I feel like all my life I've been waiting –

CON. Look! My tits are floating!

(**PRIN** *and* **FRAN** *laugh.*)

TERRI. Anyway, I'll see you guys tomorrow.

PRIN. You must kiss me first.

(**PRINCESS** *tries to grab* **TERRI***'s ankles but she gets past. She exits to her casita.*)

Shit. She's too fast for me.

FRAN. She's a fast one.

CON. I bet she is.

FRAN. Prin, she's got a nice ass.

CON. My ass used to be like that.

FRAN. Your ass? You have a baby, see what that does to your ass.

CON. Fran's body is a fucking miracle. Look at her, Prin. She is a giver and a nourisher of life. What are we? We're like...empty paper sacks.

PRIN. I'm good in the sack.

FRAN. I gotta pump soon.

PRIN. Your milk's probably 80 proof.

FRAN. Kahlua and cream.

CON. Seriously, I'm telling you. You should totally try her milk, Prin. It is incredible. It's like, what did I say, like pineapple and uh...

FRAN. What are you talking about, pineapple. Oh! I gotta take this bra off. Is Joni around here?

CON. She's probably asleep.

PRIN. She's probably on the astral plane.

FRAN. *(removing her bra)* Ah! Be free, my children.

CON. *(re: FRAN's breasts)* Look at them. My god. Aren't they beautiful, Prin?

PRIN. Beautiful, Fran. Congratulations.

FRAN. Thanks.

CON. Of woman born... Didn't Adrienne Rich write a poem about that?

PRIN. Like the cover of Jugs magazine.

CON. See, Prin, you have to mock what you don't understand. You can't just admit, "I don't understand this. This is a mystery that I cannot understand."

FRAN. Con, shut up about my tits, please. You're making them embarrassed.

CON. Shut up?

FRAN. I'm sorry.

CON. Shut up?

FRAN. *(to PRIN)* We're not supposed to say 'shut up'.

CON. Oh, I'll shut up. I'll shut up when Miss Mockety-Mock here admits that she doesn't know what she's talking about because she's never even tasted the milk.

PRIN. All right, I'll taste it.

CON. I'll get the pump. And you'll see that –

(As CON starts to pull herself out of the pool, PRIN floats over to FRAN and suckles at her breast.)

(FRAN moans.)

PRIN. Not bad. I prefer a well-made scotch, myself.

Inside Prin and Terri's Casita

(PRIN enters. TERRI is not in bed.)

PRIN. Baby?

TERRI. Here I am.

(TERRI enters.)

(PRIN lays on the bed. She pats the bed for TERRI to join her.)

PRIN. What a night, huh? I think Con and Fran are shaken up a bit.

TERRI. With the margaritas?

PRIN. No, I sucked on Fran's…uh…oh, shit. I sucked on Fran's tit.

TERRI. You did? Why?

PRIN. I don't know. Con was going on about Fran's breast milk and how holy it is and I guess it was an ounce of curiosity and a pound of shut up. I guess I had a little too much to drink.

TERRI. Wow, I've never heard you say that.

PRIN. Where are you? Why aren't you in bed with me?

(PRIN sits up. TERRI is quiet.)

PRIN. What's wrong, baby?

TERRI. I'm scared.

PRIN. Why?

TERRI. She said my mom is coming.

PRIN. Aw.

TERRI. What if it's not right? What if she comes, and I meet her, and nothing's different? I'm still lost?

PRIN. You're not lost.

TERRI. Yes, I am. I don't know this woman. She's a complete stranger to me. What if she's a waste case? Some Christian freak and she hates me…she hates you? Why do I even want to see her? She didn't want me. Why should I want her? I need my mom. I need a mom who wanted me. I am lost, Prin. I'm lost and I'm all alone.

PRIN. You're not alone. You've got me.

> (**PRIN** *holds her arms out to* **TERRI**. **TERRI** *comes to her.*)

You're my baby. You're my baby now.

TERRI. Maybe I don't need to find her.

PRIN. You should do what you need to do.

TERRI. It scares you too, doesn't it?

PRIN. Yes.

TERRI. Why?

PRIN. I don't want you to find someone you love more than me.

TERRI. That is not possible.

> (**TERRI** *kisses* **PRIN**.)

Your body, Prin. I know your body. I know it. This is my home. I love you. I love you. God, I love you.

> (**TERRI** *pushes* **PRIN** *down on her back. She kisses her way down* **PRIN**'s *body until she is between her legs.*)

Sometimes I wish I could just crawl up inside you and live there forever.

> (*As* **PRIN** *allows* **TERRI** *to go down on her, the lights flicker. A loud rumbling sound is heard. Things begin to shake. It's an earthquake.*)

PRIN. Oh, baby. See what you do to me?

> (*The shaking gets more violent until…*)

> (**TERRI**'s *painted tile falls and shatters into pieces.*)

Courtyard, Sunday, Wee Hours

*(PRIN sits in the courtyard, smoking. JONI glides in
silently and starts cleaning the pool with a net.)*

PRIN. Shit! I didn't see you there.

JONI. I am adding the chlorine. I do it now so that it will be
at a good level by the time guests are ready for a swim.

PRIN. You're on top of this place, Joni.

JONI. Mm-hm.

PRIN. Jorel and Tiny are lucky to have an employee like
you.

JONI. I tell them that.

PRIN. How long you been here? Eight? Ten years?

JONI. As long as you've been coming.

PRIN. Has it been that long? I am getting old.

JONI. We are all of us.

PRIN. You've seen me with a few different women.

JONI. Not seen, but yes. There have been a few.

PRIN. So what do you think of Terri? Pretty great, huh?

JONI. You love her a bunch.

PRIN. See, I knew you were perceptive. You're a good judge
of character, I can see that.

JONI. I'm just a blind seasonal resort manager. Nothing
more.

PRIN. This is the one, Joni. She's a keeper.

JONI. You shouldn't say things like that unless you really
mean them.

PRIN. I do. I mean it. I got her a ring.

JONI. The pool is especially murky this morning.

PRIN. Well, aren't you going to congratulate me?

JONI. Congratulations.

PRIN. Oh, by the way, that tile that you gave Terri? It fell
and broke during that tremor. Terri's heartbroken
about it. Any chance you could make her another one?

JONI. Sorry. I've given up painting.

PRIN. As of when?

JONI. Sometime earlier this evening.

PRIN. I've known you a lot of years and I still cannot figure out what makes you tick, Joni.

> *(then)*

> Hey, what'd you think about giving me one of those key readings?

JONI. Nope. Gave that up, too.

PRIN. Just now?

JONI. That's right. Okay. You should go back to bed. The shit's gonna hit the fan tomorrow and you're gonna need your sleep.

Courtyard, Sunday Afternoon

(The courtyard is empty.)

*(****CON**** enters from her casita. She is supremely hungover. She carries her* Harry Potter *book. She settles into a chair and reads.)*

*(****FRAN**** enters, sneaks up on* **CON** *and gives her a kiss on her neck.)*

CON. Don't you dare. Don't you even dare flirt with me.

FRAN. What? I thought that's what you wanted.

CON. Not after what you did last night.

FRAN. Excuse me?

CON. Don't act like you don't know what I'm talking about. You were drunk, but you weren't that drunk.

FRAN. Look, all I know is when we went to bed last night I couldn't keep my hands off you and you pushed me away. I was ready last night, sweetheart. Where were you?

CON. Gee, I don't know. Maybe I was lost in the thought of Prin sucking on your tits.

FRAN. Yeah? Well, maybe I was lost there, too.

CON. You bitch!

FRAN. I'm sorry. That's not what I meant.

CON. Yes, it is. It's the first honest thing you've said all weekend.

FRAN. Oh, come on.

CON. I saw your face, Fran. I was there, remember?

FRAN. Con, she was…

CON. That face is for me, Franny. You used to make that face only for me.

FRAN. Maybe I got a little carried away. But, yes! I mean, it felt good. But –

CON. Fran, I am so upset and freaked out by you I can barely look at you. You crossed such a line last night.

FRAN. Me? You practically forced us to –

CON. I have hives. Do you see this? Here? On the inside of my elbows. You let Prin... You let her... I can't even say it. All these months and you're so sensitive I can't even touch you and you just let Prin grab you and have her way?!

FRAN. Well, maybe next time you'll think twice before pimping my milk in front of the whole world.

CON. I wasn't the one flashing my tits in Prin's face.

FRAN. So shut the fuck up about my tits then! I am so sick of you putting my tits on a pedestal.

CON. I'm not going to apologize for loving your tits! I'm your lover. I love your tits! Deal with it!

FRAN. No, you don't! You don't love my tits. You never even talked about my tits until we had Basil and after that... that's all I am to you. I never even liked having tits. If I had it my way I'd cut them off to improve my golf swing.

CON. That's sick.

FRAN. Face it. Your tit obsession has nothing to do with loving me or wanting me. It has everything to do with the fact that you couldn't get pregnant and you can't nurse Basil and you feel left out! You hate my tits, you're mad at my tits and you're mad at me for having a baby – which I did for you because I love you – and I'm tired of it. I'm sick of being blamed for everything!

CON. That's not true. That is not the least bit true. You're just saying those things so you have an excuse not to fuck me.

FRAN. You know what, Con? Why don't you just go fuck yourself?

CON. Believe me. That's what I've been doing!

(TERRI *enters the main gate, wearing a backpack, dressed for hiking.*)

TERRI. Hey, you guys.

CON & FRAN. Hey.

TERRI. The painted canyons were spectacular. And I did see a roadrunner. Can you believe it? What a great way to start off my birthday.

(*after a beat*)

CON & FRAN. Happy birthday, Terri.

TERRI. (*suspecting something*) What's going on?

CON & FRAN. Nothing.

TERRI. This doesn't have anything to do with last night, does it?

CON. What do you mean?

TERRI. Breastmilk…?

(**FRAN** *perks up, suddenly interested.*)

FRAN. Did Prin say something to you?

TERRI. She just…mentioned it…casually.

CON. Oh, crap.

FRAN. Casually? What did she say?

CON. What do you mean 'what did she say'?

FRAN. I just want to know Prin's side of it.

CON. Side? There are no sides.

(**PRIN** *enters from the casita.*)

TERRI. Hi, baby.

PRIN. Hi, baby.

(*re:* **CON** *and* **FRAN**)

Am I just hungover or do you two look especially sour this morning?

TERRI. Honey, they're not feeling too well.

PRIN. Well, I know how to fix that.

(*She pulls a silver flask out of her pocket and pours the liquor into her coffee. She offers it to* **CON**.)

PRIN. Con? Hair of the dog?

CON. (*coldly*) No, thank you.

PRIN. Franny? How about you?

FRAN. It's gotta be better than I how I feel now.

(She takes the flask and sips.)

PRIN. Shoot. I forgot the milk. Fran, can you help me out?

(PRIN holds out her coffee mug to FRAN. CON jumps up.)

CON. *(to FRAN)* I'm going in!

TERRI. Do you want me to come with you?

CON. No.

(CON exits. FRAN tries to follow.)

PRIN. What? What did I say?

Shame on the Moon (A Restaurant), Sunday Evening

(PRIN is leading TERRI to a specially decorated table that she has reserved. She has her hands over TERRI's eyes. FRAN and CON follow behind.)

TERRI. I'm going to trip!

PRIN. No, you're not. I've got you.

TERRI. Where are you taking me?

PRIN. Just be patient. And...open.

TERRI. *(opening her eyes)* Oh! It's so beautiful! Did you do this?

PRIN. Yep.

TERRI. Oh, I love it. You didn't really do this, did you?

PRIN. Sure, I did. I paid the fags who own the party company, anyway.

TERRI. Oh, it's so special. I feel so special.

(PRIN holds out TERRI's chair.)

PRIN. Birthday girl.

(TERRI sits. PRIN pulls out CON's chair.)

Ms. Lerner?

CON. *(tight-lipped)* Thank you.

PRIN. You alright, Con?

CON. Yeah, fine. I'm just a little distracted by the sound of my skin crawling.

(CON sits. PRIN starts to pull out FRAN's chair.)

FRAN. Thanks, Prin. I can do it.

PRIN. I'm just trying to make it special for everyone. Tonight's a special night.

TERRI. It's just my birthday.

PRIN. Oh, it's that and so much more.

(PRIN picks up the wine list.)

Now, I thought we'd start with an Oregon Pinot noir. That's your favorite, right, Con?

CON. I'm having soda.

(PRIN *puts down the menu.*)

PRIN. I need to say something. Last night, I did a dumb thing. I thought it didn't mean anything, but it obviously did. Besides Terri, you two are the most important people in my life and I want you to know that. I hurt you, and I'm sorry. It's the very last thing I'd ever want to do. Will you forgive me?

FRAN. Yeah. Of course.

(PRIN *reaches for* FRAN*'s hand who gives it to her. She holds her hand out to* CON.)

PRIN. Con? I'm a fuckhead, you know that.

(CON *takes* PRIN*'s hand.*)

CON. Well, since you put it that way.

PRIN. I love you both, very much.

FRAN. *(moved)* I love you, too.

CON. Me, too.

PRIN. Okay. Now, let's party.

(*They all read their menus.*)

CON. *(looking around)* It really does look great in here.

PRIN. Leave it to fags.

TERRI. I'm getting the turkey picata.

PRIN. Oh, big surprise. She always gets the turkey picata.

FRAN. What's that, picata?

TERRI. It's like lemons and capers and yum. It's so tasty.

CON. Hey, should we do presents now? I mean, our present.

PRIN. You want to do it now, hon?

TERRI. *(excited)* I guess so.

CON. Okay. Because Fran and I –

FRAN. Con, mostly.

CON. No, you helped. Well, we've been working on this for a while now.

TERRI. Oh, god. I'm nervous.

CON. Now, it's not your typical kind of present…

PRIN. Here come the dubloons.

CON. But I think, I hope, you're really going to like it.

(She pulls a large, stuffed manila envelope from her bag and places it on the table.)

TERRI. What is it?

CON. Okay. So, as you know I've been working on Basil's second parent adoption, which just annoys me to no end. I cannot believe I have to jump through all these hoops and pay all this money just to adopt my own son. But, in the process I got into a conversation with this guy from work, who, it turns out, is an adoptee and an adoption activist.

TERRI. Ooh!

CON. And he has all these special underground ways to get information and he found your birth records. Happy birthday. We got you your birth records.

TERRI. What?

CON. We haven't looked at them. You don't have to open it, either. Or if you want to put them away and open them later, that's fine too.

TERRI. I don't know. It's so big.

(to PRIN)

It's so big, honey.

FRAN. Terri, I hope it's not too weird.

TERRI. No. I just didn't expect it. It's amazing.

(turning to PRIN)

Should I open it?

PRIN. It's your call, babe.

TERRI. I can't do it.

(then, to PRIN)

Will you read it for me? Tell me what it says.

(TERRI hands PRIN the envelope.)

(They all watch as **PRIN** *opens the envelope and reads. Silence.)*

CON. What's it say?

TERRI. I can't stand it. Give it to me.

*(**TERRI** takes the file from **PRIN**.)*

My hands are all sweaty.

*(**TERRI** reads)*

OK, I was born in Michigan, not Wisconsin.

CON. You're kidding.

TERRI. A place called…Es-CAN-aba?

PRIN. *(saying it correctly)* Escanaba.

TERRI. *(repeating)* Escanaba.

CON. Imagine that. A whole different state.

TERRI. And…oh, wow. Today's not my birthday. I was born on February 28th. It's amazing.

(then)

Oh, my god. That's my birth mother's name.

CON. What is it?

TERRI. Laura Campbell. My birth mother's name is Laura Campbell. It's so – regular. You guys, thank you. This is just incredible. I think I'm going to cry.

FRAN. I hope it helps you. We didn't want to make things difficult.

TERRI. No, it's great. I've been wanting to do this but it's been hard to really take the steps and get going with everything. This is really going to help me. Though I don't really know what to do with it. It's scary and great at the same time.

CON. I'm so glad, Ter. I know how much this means to you.

*(**TERRI** snuggles up to **PRIN**.)*

TERRI. Honey, are you alright?

*(**PRIN** pulls away from **TERRI**.)*

PRIN. I'm fine.

*(**PRIN** puts her hand to her forehead.)*

CON. No, you're not. You look horrible.

PRIN. Too much sun, I guess. Let's get some drinks. Where's that waitress? Jesus Christ, haven't we been here like an hour?

TERRI. Calm down, Prin. We've only been here like a minute.

PRIN. Well, we don't fucking have our drinks and we've been here long enough for that.

TERRI. All right. Geez, you bear.

PRIN. It's your birthday dinner. I paid a lot of fucking money for this and I expect fucking decent service.

TERRI. Well, it's not my birthday, really.

(PRIN slams her fist on the table.)

PRIN. It is. Today is your birthday. That is what we know.

FRAN. P, calm down. The waitress is coming.

PRIN. Yeah, sorry. I just want everything to be right.

TERRI. Honey, you know if you're not feeling well…

(PRIN escapes TERRI's caress and picks up her menu.)

PRIN. *(cold, distant)* No. I'll be fine. I just need to figure out what I want.

(FRAN and CON work to relieve the tension.)

FRAN. You know what they say about hot-headed people. They got cold feet!

CON. I have to admit, Terri. I don't think Prin ever loved anyone the way she loves you.

TERRI. *(to PRIN)* Is that true?

PRIN. Yes.

FRAN. Hey, Prin. I think now would be the perfect time to give Terri her "boat," don't you?

(TERRI and CON laugh. They all look at PRIN, expectant.)

(PRIN gives TERRI nothing.)

PRIN. Shall we order?

(PRIN signals for the waitress.)

Cockatiels, a Night Club, Later that Night

(Thumping music plays.)

TERRI. We didn't have to come here.

PRIN. It's your birthday.

TERRI. Let's just go home.

PRIN. We can't do that.

TERRI. Look, I know you're upset.

(TERRI reaches for PRIN. PRIN jumps up.)

PRIN. I'm not upset. Everything's great. We need some drinks.

(She goes to the bar.)

FRAN. *(trying to make light, re: the music)* I know this one. This is Beyoncé, right babe?

TERRI. What should I do?

CON. You're fine, sweetie.

FRAN. She's moody. You know that.

TERRI. Excuse me.

(TERRI exits.)

CON. What is Prin doing?

FRAN. I don't know. She's freaking me out, though.

CON. Maybe she really can't do this commitment thing.

FRAN. She seemed so clear and calm about it the other day.

CON. I know, but this is Prin we're talking about. Maybe she could imagine it in theory but the real thing is giving her a melt down – oh, here she comes. Hey, Prin, how're you doing?

(PRIN returns with a pitcher of daiquiris.)

PRIN. Great.

FRAN. Since when do you drink daiquiris?

PRIN. Terri loves 'em. Plus, I slipped the guy an extra twenty to put in the good stuff.

(She drinks.)

Almost drinkable.

FRAN. You nervous about the...you know?

PRIN. The what?

FRAN. The ring.

PRIN. Oh. That.

CON. This is a big step for you, commitment and everything.

PRIN. You guys act like you invented matrimony.

FRAN. I don't think that's what Con's saying, P.

PRIN. Well, you didn't. People have been clinging desperately to each other since Adam and Eve. Or Adam and Steve.

FRAN. We're just saying calm down. You're acting weird.

(*TERRI returns.*)

PRIN. Daiquiris, Terri.

TERRI. No, thank you.

PRIN. I got them for you. For your birthday.

TERRI. I don't feel like drinking.

PRIN. Don't be a bitch, Terri.

(*TERRI drinks.*)

That's better. You guys too. We're all going to have fun tonight.

(*All drink quietly.*)

Yeah. This place is hopping tonight. Pedro's here.

(*She waves.*)

Hey, Pedro! What a great guy. Pedro! Man!

(*to* TERRI)

So, how's it feel to be thirty-seven? Thirty-seven is a special birthday. I got you a special present for your special birthday.

TERRI. You don't have to get me anything...

PRIN. 'Course I do. That wouldn't be right, not giving you something. Tonight, you get to have a special party. A private party. With whoever you want.

FRAN. Princess...

PRIN. So, who do you like?

TERRI. I like you.

PRIN. *(harsh)* That's not what I mean. I mean out there. Who do you like here?

TERRI. I don't understand.

CON. You are not going to play that juvenile –

PRIN. You can sit it out, Con. This is Terri's present.

TERRI. I don't want to play.

PRIN. You saying you don't like my present?

CON. She doesn't want to play, Prin.

PRIN. *(to* **CON***)* What are you, her–?

(to **TERRI***)*

Who do you like, Terri?

CON. *(scanning the crowd)* All right. Since we seem to have to do whatever Princess wants tonight…I like Black Baseball Cap.

FRAN. Her? What is it about you and women with facial hair?

CON. Maybe you should grow a moustache and find out.

PRIN. *(ignoring them)* Who do you like, Terri?

TERRI. Can we please not do this?

*(***PRIN*** notices someone in the crowd.)*

PRIN. Here we go. Baby butch in the corner. You think she's hot, right?

TERRI. No.

PRIN. Sure you do. Go for it, Ter. I won't be mad.

TERRI. I don't want to go for it.

PRIN. Well, I want you to go for it.

TERRI. You're not my master.

PRIN. No? I pay for your car, the insurance. I pay for your haircuts. For that bullshit degree you're about to get. For your therapist so you can cry out some sob story about your mommy.

CON. Jesus Christ, Prin, cool it.

PRIN. I want my money's worth.

CON. You're being an asshole.

PRIN. *(to CON)* Just 'cause you're all dried up doesn't mean the rest of us can't get laid.

TERRI. Okay, Prin. You're right, she is hot. Fuck you.

(TERRI gathers her things and leaves the table. They watch her go.)

PRIN. That didn't take much, did it?

CON. You are really a piece of work, you know that?

(CON gets up and leaves.)

FRAN. *(after CON)* Honey–!

(to PRIN)

I know you're freaked. But don't do this. Don't do what you always do!

PRIN. Do you think you could handle getting your nose out of my fucking business?

FRAN. I'm just trying to help you.

PRIN. Go run after your wife! You do everything else she says.

FRAN. Fuck this. No. I'm fucking sick of this. You act like you know everything and I'm just some pussy-whipped dope.

PRIN. You said it.

FRAN. I thought you were going to do it. But you're fucking everything up. Yeah, me and Con we don't fuck all the time like you guys. But there's more to love than sex. Con, Basil, they make my life all worth it. I'm not going to apologize for that.

PRIN. Then go! Be with your beautiful family.

FRAN. I won't stand for you talking to Con like that.

PRIN. So?

FRAN. What the fuck am I even doing here with you?

(FRAN leaves.)

(PRIN drinks.)

Palm Canyon Drive

(*FRAN runs to catch up with* CON.)

FRAN. Wait up! Con!

(*then, breathing heavily*)

I couldn't run…flip-flops.

CON. I could just kill her. She is a goddamned bully.

FRAN. She's acting all weird. I tried to talk to her. She wouldn't. I think Terri went with that girl.

CON. Shit. Prin is so fucking selfish.

FRAN. You okay? I told her, she can't talk to you like that.

CON. You did?

FRAN. Hell, yeah.

CON. Oh, Fran.

FRAN. She can't treat my baby like that.

CON. I don't want to be dried up, Fran. I don't. I want to be loose and sexy like we used to be.

FRAN. I know, baby. I'm sorry.

CON. God, do we have to be in some sick relationship in order to have sex? Can you be in a normal relationship where you love each other and respect each other and still want to fuck?

FRAN. I don't know, baby.

CON. Yes. Just say yes, you dummy.

FRAN. Yes, yes. Yes, we can. I love you, Con.

CON. I love you, too.

(*They embrace. They start to kiss. Pecks turn to soul kisses.*)

We gotta hurry!

Courtyard, Monday, Pre-Dawn

(**PRINCESS** *sits on a chaise with a cigarette and a bottle of Jack Daniels by her side, so wasted she neither smokes nor drinks.*)

Fran and Con's Casita

(FRAN *and* CON *are naked in bed.*)

CON. What do you think Devra would say about that?

FRAN. I think she'd say we're cured.

CON. Maybe we better not tell her.

FRAN. She might be upset that she's not going to get to see us every week.

CON. Or get our $200 a session.

FRAN. Poor Devra.

CON. I feel sorry for her.

FRAN. But not too sorry.

(CON *rolls on top of* FRAN *and they begin to make love all over again.*)

Courtyard

(The Main Gate creaks open. TERRI enters.)

TERRI. I'm back.

PRIN. How was she?

TERRI. Great.

PRIN. I packed your bag. The keys are on the table. Take the Lexus. You can have it. I'll stay here a few days. Give you a chance to clear your shit out.

TERRI. You want me to leave?

PRIN. Forget it. You keep the house. I'll get my stuff some other time.

TERRI. Do you not love me any more?

PRIN. Last night was a test, and you failed. Or passed, depending on how you look at it.

TERRI. What did I do? Did I do something to make you mad? I thought you were happy.

PRIN. I thought I was happy, too. But now that I see you're ready to jump into bed with the first girl who comes around…

TERRI. You made me do that!

PRIN. *(shaking TERRI violently)* Did I have a fucking gun to your head?

(PRIN hurls TERRI to the ground.)

TERRI. I didn't fuck her. I didn't fuck her. I was so mad at you, I wanted to. Just to show you. To hurt you. But I couldn't. I kept seeing you. Wanting to feel you.

PRIN. Shut up! Stop talking! Take the keys and get out!

(In their casita, FRAN and CON look up from their love-making.)

CON. Is that Prin and Terri?

(They sit up and listen, trying to make out the words.)

TERRI. You're drinking too much.

PRIN. You don't get to tell me how much I'm drinking!

CON. What the hell?

FRAN. She's drunk.

TERRI. My god, we love each other. I know you love me. How can you just let me go? How can you do that?

PRIN. I had to.

(whimpering)

I tried to do the right thing.

TERRI. Prin, I love you. Please! Just let me hold you and you'll know!

(PRIN balls her hand into a fist then whirls around and punches TERRI in the face.)

(TERRI shrieks in pain.)

PRIN. Don't you touch me!

FRAN. Holy shit!

(TERRI runs out of the courtyard.)

(FRAN leaps out of bed, naked, and runs into the courtyard.)

CON. What's going on?

(CON follows FRAN, wrapping herself in the sheet, but can't keep going because the sheet is still tucked in.)

(FRAN enters the courtyard just as the Main Gate is closing behind TERRI.)

FRAN. Prin? What the fuck?

PRIN. Go back to bed.

FRAN. What just happened?

PRIN. You're naked.

FRAN. *(calling to CON)* Gimme a towel, babe.

CON. *(from inside the casita)* What's going on out there?

FRAN. *(to PRIN)* Sit down, pal.

PRIN. I don't need to sit.

(She stumbles, almost falls.)

I'm going to bed.

FRAN. No, Prin. What the fuck just happened?

PRIN. Terri and I just broke up. Go to bed.

FRAN. Your hand is bleeding.

PRIN. *(seeing it for the first time)* Oh. I caught her tooth.

FRAN. Did you hit her?

PRIN. I hit her in the face. I hate her. Go back to bed.

FRAN. What the fuck did you do, Prin?

CON. I'm going to find her.

> (**CON** *exits to the bathroom to get dressed.*)

FRAN. You are fucked up, Prin. I can't believe this.

PRIN. *She* messed around on *me!*

FRAN. You are insane.

PRIN. What did I do?

FRAN. Good god, Prin.

PRIN. I broke my rule. I broke my 15-year rule, man.

FRAN. Why do you do this?

PRIN. I can't change it.

FRAN. That's bullshit. We make choices.

PRIN. I choose oblivion.

> (**PRIN** *grabs her bottle of Jack Daniels.*)
>
> (**FRAN** *exits to her casita.*)
>
> (**PRINCESS** *ponders the water, then slowly walks into the pool, fully clothed.*)
>
> (*She sinks below the surface.*)
>
> (*A long beat before…*)
>
> (**JONI** *enters with a pool net on a long pole. She starts cleaning the pool. She feels something at the bottom of the shallow end. She prods her with the net.*)
>
> (**PRIN** *comes up, gasping for air, spitting water.*)

JONI. What are you doing down there?

PRIN. I was looking for a hair tie.

JONI. Your hair's short.

PRIN. Not my hair tie, some girl's hair tie. Some girl with long hair.

(*JONI returns to cleaning the pool.*)

(**PRINCESS** *sits on the edge, soaking wet. Her bottle of Jack Daniels is filled with pool water. She pours it back into the pool.*)

Do you have kids, Joni?

JONI. I have a boy. He'd be 42.

PRIN. What happened?

JONI. He was riding a motorcycle in Banff National Park. You ever been there?

PRIN. No. Just Vancouver.

JONI. It's beautiful country. I get up there every summer. On the off season. He was riding a Nighthawk 650. I'd got it for him the summer before. Man, he loved that bike. And, of course, being a kid, he thought he could do anything and never have to pay. He hit a patch of oil and flew right off the edge of the mountain. They never even found his body. I like to think a cougar got it. He would've liked that.

PRIN. How old was he?

JONI. Nineteen. (*pause*) You?

PRIN. Just the one.

JONI. You love her very much.

PRIN. I never loved anything so much.

(*pause*)

Ain't it a pisser? I let one guy fuck me, for like two seconds, and I'm pregnant. It's ironic. But then, I come from a long line of fertile women. Stu. What a fucking idiot. Every bad quality she has, that's where it comes from. It was his girlfriend I loved. She was so beautiful. You know how the chicks were then? Hair all crazy. No bras. That was a good time for womanhood. I would've done anything for her. I did. So, I'm knocked up and she and Stu are in Mexico with my money. What am I going to do? Raise this baby? I wanted her to have an OK life. Not scrounging around on the streets. And she did. She had a good life. She complains about it but it was good. Maybe it can still be good.

(pause)

PRIN. *(cont.)* What's the biggest mistake you ever made?

JONI. *(She ponders this for a long while.)* Not buying that laundromat when I had the money.

(pause)

You?

PRIN. Not getting two bottles of Jack while the liquor store was still open.

JONI. Ho.

*(**PRINCESS** lies back on the cement. **JONI** exits.)*

Courtyard, Later that Morning

(**PRIN** *lays in the courtyard.*)

(**FRAN** *crosses from her casita to the main gate carrying packed suitcases. She opens the gate and* **CON** *enters.*)

FRAN. Is Terri okay?

CON. No. I told her to wait in the car. I'm gonna get her things.

(**TERRI** *appears in the doorway and walks past* **CON** *and* **FRAN.**)

FRAN. Terri.

CON. Terri don't.

(**TERRI** *approaches* **PRIN.**)

TERRI. Con told me about the ring. I had a feeling... You don't have to do that. You don't have to say anything or do anything you don't want to do.

PRIN. Con. Get her out of my sight.

CON. Terri.

(**CON** *tries to get* **TERRI.**)

(**TERRI** *evades* **CON** *and prostrates herself before* **PRIN**, *not daring to touch her.*)

TERRI. Prin, please. Please, don't make me go. Don't leave me. I'll be good. I'm promise. I'll be good.

(**TERRI** *takes down her dress, exposing her breasts.*)

You want me. I know you want me. I'm beautiful. I know I'm beautiful to you.

(*She puts* **PRIN**'*s hands on her own breasts.*)

TERRI. Tell me you don't want me.

PRIN. I don't want you. Not like that.

TERRI. Why, Prin? Why do you hate me? Why are you doing this to me? Why?

PRIN. You don't want to know!

TERRI. Tell me, Prin. Tell me. I'm breaking apart.

PRIN. We can never see each other again.

TERRI. No. No. I can't breathe. I can't see. Nobody wants me. Nobody ever wanted me. Nobody ever will.

PRIN. I wanted you.

TERRI. Liar.

PRIN. Thirty-seven years ago. But I gave you up.

TERRI. No.

PRIN. I am Laura Campbell.

FRAN. Oh, god.

CON. No.

TERRI. You're not! Prin, stop it.

PRIN. I am your mother.

TERRI. Stop it! Stop it! You hate me! Why do you hate me!?

(PRIN steps toward TERRI.)

PRIN. Terri –

TERRI. No! It's not true!

PRIN. Terri…

FRAN. *(protecting TERRI)* Get away from her, you!

PRIN. I didn't know!

FRAN. A mother knows. A mother always knows.

(PRIN lets out a yowl.)

PRIN. That's my daughter!

(PRIN tries to get to TERRI. FRAN holds her back.)

FRAN. Prin!

CON. Stop!

(PRIN breaks free of FRAN's grasp. And moves toward TERRI.)

(TERRI backs away, afraid.)

TERRI. No! No!

(TERRI cowers.)

PRIN. I'm a monster.

(PRIN collapses. Sobs.)

My baby, my baby, my baby…

CON. Prin…

FRAN. Let her be.

CON. It's too much.

PRIN. What did I do to my baby?

> (*Now* **TERRI** *stands before* **PRIN.**)

TERRI. Tell me my birth story.

> (*silence*)

FRAN. (*harshly*) Tell her.

CON. (*kindly*) Prin, tell her.

PRIN. I was alone. I walked into St. Francis Hospital and they undressed me and left me in some cold room. Nobody helped me. The nurses were talking in the hall, saying they'd let nature take its course. I pushed all day and all night until you tore your way out of me.

TERRI. Did you hold me?

PRIN. No.

TERRI. Did you want me?

PRIN. No. Not at first. But as you grew inside me, oh, I got real soft for you. I would've kept you if I could.

TERRI. You didn't.

PRIN. You were better off without me.

CON. This is your mother.

TERRI. What now? What now, Prin?

PRIN. I can't lose you again.

> (*They move toward each other. They almost kiss.* **TERRI** *recoils.*)

TERRI. No.

> (**PRIN** *grabs* **TERRI***'s hands.*)

PRIN. Please. I can't live without you.

TERRI. I can't be your baby. Not anymore. Let go of my hands.

> (**PRIN** *releases* **TERRI**. **TERRI** *goes to* **CON** *and* **FRAN.**)

PRIN. Terri.

*(*TERRI *turns to* PRIN.*)*

PRIN. You turned out good.

TERRI. I did.

(The three exit. The wind starts to blow. JONI *enters and closes the doors.)*

JONI. Didn't see it coming, did you?

*(*PRIN *shakes her head.)*

The End

ABOUT THE PLAYWRIGHTS

THE FIVE LESBIAN BROTHERS are Maureen Angelos, Babs Davy, Dominique Dibbell, Peg Healey and Lisa Kron. The Brothers came together as a theater company in 1989 after performing together in various other combinations at the Obie award–winning WOW Cafe Theatre in New York City's East Village.

Together the Brothers have written five plays, *Voyage to Lesbos* (1990), *Brave Smiles* (1992), *The Secretaries* (1994), *Brides of the Moon* (1996), and *Oedipus at Palm Springs* (2006), which was written by Maureen Angelos, Dominique Dibbell, Peg Healey, and Lisa Kron.

The Brothers' work has been presented Off-Broadway and Off-Off Broadway by New York Theatre Workshop, the Joseph Papp Public Theatre, the WOW Cafe Theatre, Downtown Art Company, Performance Space 122, Dixon Place, La Mama, the Kitchen, and the Whitney Museum of American Art at Phillip Morris. They have toured to London, Los Angeles, San Francisco, San Diego, Houston, Columbus, Seattle, Philadelphia, Boston, and the deep woods of Michigan. Their plays have also been produced by other companies throughout the United States and, believe it or not, in Zagreb, Croatia.

The Brothers are the recipients of a Village Voice Obie Award, a New York Dance and Performance Award ("Bessie"), a GLAAD Media Award, and a New York Press Award as Best Performance Group. An anthology of their plays entitled *Five Lesbian Brothers/Four Plays* was published in 2000 by Theatre Communications Group and was nominated for a Lambda Literary award.

Also by
The Five Lesbian Brothers...

Brave Smiles

Brides of the Moon

The Secretaries

Voyage to Lesbos

OTHER TITLES AVAILABLE FROM SAMUEL FRENCH

BRAVE SMILES

The Five Lesbian Brothers
Maureen Angelos, Babs Davy, Dominique Dibbell,
Peg Healey and Lisa Kron

Comedy / 5f

In *Brave Smiles…another lesbian tragedy,* master satirists The Five
Lesbian Brothers turn their merciless eyes on the history of lesbians in theater, film, and literature. From their dismal yet erotical-
ly charged beginnings at the orphanage under the grip of a sadis-
tic headmistress, our five heroines cross continents and a century
to face their absurdly tragic ends. Along the way, they experience
alcoholism, suicide, loneliness, pill popping, blacklisting, and a
malignant brain tumor. Students of the lesbian art of misery will
recognize gleeful skewerings of *The Well of Loneliness, The Group,
Maedchen in Uniform,* and *The Children's Hour* in this rollicking,
hilarious, and smart multicharacter classic.

"Smart, satirical farce that uses laughter and touches of raunchy
humor to debunk the myth of the doomed lesbian."
– *The New York Times*

"Parodies gay clichés about lesbian destiny with deadly accuracy."
–*LA Times*

OTHER TITLES AVAILABLE FROM SAMUEL FRENCH

THE SECRETARIES

The Five Lesbian Brothers
Maureen Angelos, Babs Davy, Dominique Dibbell,
Peg Healey and Lisa Kron

Comedy-horror / 5f (with doubling)

Something's rotten in Big Bone! Pretty Patty Johnson is thrilled to join the secretarial pool at the Cooney Lumber Mill under the iron-fisted leadership of sultry office manager Susan Curtis. But she soon begins to feel that all is not right—the enforced diet of Slim-Fast shakes, the strange clicking language between the girls, the monthly disappearance of a lumberjack. By the time Patty discovers murder is part of these office killers' skill set, it's too late to turn back! In the guise of satiric exploitation-horror, *The Secretaries* takes an unflinching look at the warping cultural expectations of femininity.

"*The Secretaries* is a sustained, amusing look at the fine line between aggression and assertiveness."
– *The New Yorker*

"The Five Lesbian Brothers render their satirical portraits with a deft but merciless eye."
– *L.A. Times*

"95 minutes of gritty, bawdy, bloody humor pregnant with incisive social commentary."
– *San Francisco Examiner*

"A mordantly cheerful slice of Grand Guignol."
–*New York Times*

OTHER TITLES AVAILABLE FROM SAMUEL FRENCH

KICKASS PLAYS FOR WOMEN

Jane Shepard

Drama / 2f per play / Unit Set

Award-winning new playwright Jane Shepard comes to print with four powerful short plays for women. Edgy, original, and with a darkly funny humanity, here are four pieces that give new muscle to actresses, providing roles of exceptional range. All successfully produced on the New York stage, each play features two-woman casts, with age-open roles, in work that explores our tender, brave, and some-times brutal search for meaning. Includes both comedy and drama, with a variety of settings and running times. An excellent introduction to the playwright, *KickAss Plays For Women* is a vital text for actresses of any age, or anyone hungry for compelling new plays.

Nine (2f) Two women held in a life-threatening situation and the mind games they play to keep one another alive. Held in a cell and chained apart, their only currency is words, and balance of power is everything when a single word becomes the hanging point between life and death.

Commencing (2f) The beautiful Kelli can't wait for the blind date her friends have set her up on. Until it turns out to be one very disappointed lesbian named Arlin. Mutually appalled, yet appallingly intrigued, they proceed to pull the screws loose on both straight and gay women's culture, to find the common ground beneath in the search for love & self.

Friend of the Deceased (2f) An embittered widow lies in wait at her husband's grave for the appearance his mistress, and encounters a soul-ful teen. Unable to extract a confession from the girl, the widow offers to buy one, and finds that she has purchased a deeper truth.

The Last Nickel (2f and 2 puppeteers) Theatrical, funny & touching, It's an-other long night for Jamie, with an obnoxious sister & a trio of sardonic puppets to keep her awake. Tinged with fun & sisterly nostalgia, the mer-riment comes inevitably to focus on the cause of Jamie's self destruction, and the loss that has brought her to the edge.

OTHER TITLES AVAILABLE FROM SAMUEL FRENCH

DEVIL BOYS FROM BEYOND

Buddy Thomas and Kenneth Elliott
Based on an original script by Buddy Thomas
Original song, "Sensitive Girl", music and lyrics by Drew Fornarola

Comedy / 4m, 4f / Unit Set

Flying Saucers! Backstabbing Bitches! Muscle Hunks and Men in Pumps! Wake up and smell the alien invasion in this outrageous comedy by the author of the off-Broadway hit play, *Crumple Zone*.

"***** [FIVE STARS]! Buddy Thomas's deliriously campy sci-fi spoof—one of the most entertaining shows I have ever seen at the Fringe Festival—is naughty, gleeful fun...The show opens a fabulous portal to the past: not just the paranoid world of the 1950s, but the legendary drag romps of Charles Ludlam's Ridiculous Theatrical Company and Charles Busch's Theatre-in-Limbo from the 1960s through the 1980s. *Devil Boys from Beyond* is a necklace of golden links to that wild theatrical tradition. If there were any justice in this mixed-up world of ours, the whole show would be tractor-beamed Off Broadway tomorrow."
— *Adam Feldman, Time Out New York*

"Cheap in all the right ways, the fast, taw dry and very funny *Devil Boys From Beyond* is the Fringe Festival at its best."
— *New York Post*

"*Devil Boys From Beyond* is how a no-budget show should be done...an uproarious homage to C-movies and the golden age of camp!"
—*Back Stage*